M000158343

THE ISLAND RETREAT

Getaway Bay, Book 4

ELANA JOHNSON

feel-good fiction

ELANA JOHNSON

Copyright © 2021 by Elana Johnson

All rights reserved.

No part of this book may be reproduced in any form or by any
electronic or mechanical means, including information storage and
retrieval systems, without written permission from the author, except for
the use of brief quotations in a book review.

ISBN-13: 978-1638760061

Chapter One

"All right, guys." Shannon Bell put her purse over her shoulder and clicked her way toward the front door. "Be good while I'm at work." She flashed a bright smile to her two cats, both of whom sat at perfect attention a few feet away.

Of course, neither of them responded to her, and Shannon went out the door and down the steps. She had a routine she followed each morning, and she was right on schedule to hit Roasted at their slowest time between eight and nine.

She'd tried different times, and eight-twenty in the morning seemed to be the best time to get her daily dose of caffeine before she had to go to work at Your Tidal Forever. She loved her job, though it was a bit intense from time to time.

"At least the celebrity wedding and the royal wedding are over," she told herself as she buckled her seatbelt and started her car. She loved this car, and she lowered the top to let in the spring sunshine as she started toward downtown Getaway Bay.

She hooked her purse over her arm as she walked into the coffee shop, running her fingers through her hair to tame some of the messy curls back into waves. Only four people waited in line, and Shannon smiled to herself that she'd timed her coffee shop visit exactly right again.

Shannon prided herself on the details of things. It was what made her a good secretary, and why Hope Sorensen at Your Tidal Forever had told Shannon she could never quit.

Her body was still recovering from the high-profile weddings over the past couple of months, and she wished she wasn't such a night owl. That, or she needed another job where she didn't have to be to work by nine.

But she had a secretarial degree and a professional certification in organization. So she was well-suited for the many moving parts a wedding planning business required, and she'd enjoyed her last five years at Your Tidal Forever.

Well, most of the time she enjoyed the work. Sometimes Hope could be a little intense, and when they had two of the biggest celebrities tying the knot one month, and then a prince getting married only a couple later, there had been times that Shannon felt like she'd lose her mind with all the tiny pieces that needed to be finished on time.

In the five minutes she waited to put in her order for

a large caramel mocha, the bell on the door rang eight more times, and she asked for a cranberry orange bran muffin too, as she rarely ate breakfast before she left the house.

With summer right around the corner, Shannon had dozens of tasks to be completed that day, and she'd be lucky if she got fifteen minutes for lunch. Maybe she could get Riley to get food for everyone, or she'd just run down the boardwalk to the Ohana Resort, which had recently opened a shop that served soups, salads, and sandwiches for the professional lunch crowd. The Lunch Spot promised food in ten minutes or less, and they had dozens of tables in the sand that always seemed full.

She got her coffee and turned to leave. Her eyes scanned the line of people waiting, catching on a tall, good-looking man she'd seen every day for a long time. She couldn't pinpoint when she'd first met Doctor Jeremiah Yeates, or when she'd learned his name, or when she'd realized that he worked in the building just down from Your Tidal Forever.

It seemed like they'd known each other for a while, and she waved to him as she passed.

"You beat me today," he said with a smile, and she couldn't help the little laugh that came out of her mouth. She quelled it by sipping her coffee, because while she and Jeremiah were friendly, there had never been much of a spark there.

She knew his name and where he worked. That was all. They could probably ride to work together if they

3

wanted to, but neither of them had ever brought it up. And Shannon wasn't going to today either.

Yes, Jeremiah was handsome and clearly well-off, as Shannon never saw him wearing anything but an expensive suit, and she'd seen him when he got to Roasted before her—he bought coffee for his whole office.

Every morning, the man bought coffee for his whole office. Shannon couldn't even imagine Hope doing that, though the owner did sometimes bring in food, but usually for clients and the employees just ate what was left over.

As Shannon walked across the parking lot to her car, her purse swinging and the coffee in her hand a bit too warm to really drink. Shannon was more of a lukewarm coffee lover, and she probably wouldn't touch her brew for another hour at least.

She found a couple standing at the front corner of her car, and she glanced at the man, a blip of anxiety flipping through her. She clicked her keys to unlock the car, though the top on the convertible was still down and if there had been anything worth stealing inside, it probably would've been gone by now.

The couple moved away, and Shannon glanced at the front of her beloved car. It was fine. Of course it was fine. Getaway Bay didn't have a high crime rate, and Shannon didn't really have anything to be worried about.

Except the flat tire staring back at her.

"Oh, no," she said, the words part of a much larger moan. She opened the door and put her purse inside, as well as her coffee. Then she placed her hands on her hips and faced the tire. Her father had taught her how to change a flat tire, as well as her oil, but Shannon never used the lessons. She had money, and why should she shimmy under her car when Max could do it at the lube shop for thirty bucks?

But Max wasn't here now, and Shannon had a ton to do at work. She opened her trunk and pulled back the roof to reveal the spare tire. She had no idea if she had the right tools to change a tire, but she was going to find out.

She found an X-shaped tool that she seemed to recall her father using to loosen the bolts. Bolts? That didn't seem like the right term, but Shannon literally made appointments, took messages, and tasted wedding cakes for a living.

The tool fit over the bolts, and she twisted. Nothing happened. After several more minutes of straining and trying to get even one of those stupid bolts off, sweat poured down Shannon's face. Her blouse had come untucked and she had no idea where her heels were.

She crouched next to the tire, frustration about to make her say or do something she'd likely regret later—like calling her father for help.

"Can't do it," she said, and she also regretted her skirt choice, as this one was a little snug along her waist and hips.

"Need some help?" a man asked, and Shannon startled toward the deep, familiar voice. She twisted and peered up at none other than Jeremiah Yeates and the two trays of coffee he held in his hands.

"I have a flat tire," she said, trying to straighten.

Horror struck her like lightning at the sound of a seam *riiipping*, and she spun to put her backside against her cherry red convertible.

To Jeremiah's great credit, he acted like she hadn't just split her skirt open and stepped over to the hood of the car, where he set down the seven cups of coffee. "I think I can change a tire."

"I haven't been able to get off the bolts," she said, wiping her bangs off her forehead. Her hand came away wet, and more embarrassment squirreled through her.

"Let's see what I can do with these lug nuts," Jeremiah said, taking his suit coat off and draping it over the driver's side door. He wore a light blue, short-sleeved dress shirt, and Shannon couldn't help but admire the width of his shoulders and the obvious strength in his biceps.

Shannon looked away, her heart pounding a bit harder than normal for a reason she couldn't identify. So Jeremiah spent some time in the gym. So did a lot of men.

He picked up the tool she'd been wrestling with and crouched where she'd been. With the first yank on the wrench, the bolt—lug nut, whatever—came loose, and Shannon felt another blast of humiliation.

Jeremiah made short work of the lug nuts and pulled

the full-size tire off. "Yeah, it looks like you drove over a nail," he said.

"Oh," she said. "I live over in the Cliff Cove area, and they're doing some construction up there."

"Yeah," he said with a big grin. "I live up there too."

Surprise pulled through her. "You do?"

"Yeah, off White Sails Lane."

That was only a few blocks from her, and she said, "I'm off Five Island."

His smile was glorious and beautiful, and why hadn't Shannon ever noticed it before? She tucked her dark hair behind her ear, wishing the sun didn't make her whole head feel like it was ablaze.

"I'm going to be so late for work," she said. "I'm so sorry. Are you—do you have a patient this morning?"

"I'm okay," he said, walking to the back of the car to get the spare tire. "Let me text my secretary real quick." He pulled his phone out and started sending a message, prompting Shannon to do the same thing. Hope couldn't blame her for being late if she had a flat tire. In fact, Shannon beat Hope to the office every day anyway.

"Shannon?" he asked from the trunk, and Shannon looked up from her phone.

"Yeah?"

"I don't think this spare is any good." He glanced at her and back into the trunk.

She shimmied along the side of the car and placed her palm flat against her backside as she turned to stand right beside him. She peered into the trunk too, asking, "What's wrong with it?"

"Look how it's cracked along the side there?" He ran his finger along the edge of the tire. "We can't put this on."

She appreciated the use of "we," but she had absolutely no idea what to do now.

"I can give you a ride to work," he said. "And maybe you can call someone to come tow the car and get the tire fixed?" He looked at her like she had resources to do that. And she did, but she didn't want to call her dad and admit she couldn't change her own tire.

"All right," she said. "Are you sure it's okay?"

Jeremiah grinned at her. "It's no problem, Shannon," he said. "We work right next door to each other, and I just found out you're like, three blocks away from where I live." He hefted the flat tire into her trunk and slammed it closed. "So it's absolutely no problem."

Shannon couldn't help returning his smile, because it was just so dashing, and he was so good-looking, and he smelled like cologne and sunshine and dark roast coffee.

As she collected her purse and coffee and walked with him over to his car, Shannon wondered why she'd never looked at Doctor Jeremiah Yeates more than once on her way out of the coffee shop.

Chapter Two

Jeremiah's heart pounced around his chest as the blocks passed from Roasted to Shannon's house, and then from there to the boardwalk where his practice sat next to Your Tidal Forever.

Just ask her, he told himself for probably the tenth time.

He'd always found Shannon Bell to be beautiful, exotic almost, and completely out of his reach. She wore blouses with flamingoes or horses or pineapples on them. She wore black or navy pencil skirts, or sometimes long, flowy dresses that brushed the sidewalk. If she wore pants, they were slacks, and he wondered what she'd look like in a pair of skinny jeans.

No, he told himself, banishing the fantasies from his mind. He barely knew Shannon, though he'd seen her in line at the coffee shop for years now. The day he'd realized she worked at Your Tidal Forever, a mere twenty feet from his office, had been a great one.

But had he done anything about his casual friendship with the lovely Shannon Bell?

Nope.

Absolutely not.

Because Jeremiah had spent a year getting over his fiancée and then he wasn't sure how to ask Shannon out after twelve months of quick smiles and nods in the coffee line.

And now she was in his car, those black waves cascading over her shoulders and the scent of her fruity perfume seeping into the leather seats.

"So," he said, wondering how he could learn more about her in the short time they'd be in the car together. "How long have you lived on Five Island Street?"

"Oh, about three years now," she said, glancing at him. "You?"

"I've been there for a decade," he said. "It's a nice area." He wanted to drive into the nearest lamppost so he wouldn't have to continue this lame conversation.

"It is," she said. "Are you from the island?"

"Yep," he said, popping the P. "Sure am. I have one sister, and my parents live in the older area of the island at the end of Main Street." He glanced at her. "They're getting up there in age."

"They are?" She looked fully at him now. "How old are you?"

"Thirty-nine," he said. "My parents were both forty when they had me."

If she was surprised by that, she didn't show it. "Younger sister, huh?"

"Yeah, she's a synchronized swimmer. You ever been to any of the shows on the island?"

Shannon shook her head, and he wondered if she did more than work and get coffee in the mornings.

"What about you?" he asked. "Siblings? Oldest? Youngest?"

"I'm the oldest. Two sisters. My parents live out on the highway toward the cattle ranch. Have for decades." She nodded and nodded, and Jeremiah could sense her discomfort. So he definitely wasn't going to be asking her to be his date to the recognition gala. But he *needed* a date....

He pulled into the parking lot the wedding planning place shared with his office, his time with Shannon coming to an end. "So," he said. "This might be totally crazy, but the City Council is having this…thing that I have to go to, and I need a date. Are you busy next weekend?"

Shannon blinked, her deep, brown eyes soaking him up. Jeremiah let her too, and he wished his crush on this woman wasn't quite so large. "Next weekend?" she asked. "Friday or Saturday?"

"It's on Saturday night," he said.

"And it's a…thing?" Her eyes smiled at him, and he

wondered if this was flirting. He wasn't sure, because he hadn't been out with anyone since Elaine, and she'd taken most of his heart with her when she'd left Getaway Bay.

"It's a…dinner and a program," he said. "The city is recognizing me for my work with kids." He hated saying it out loud, but she'd asked.

"You're getting the Getaway Bay Professional Dignitary Award?" Her eyes widened, and she leaned away from him and folded her arms. Jeremiah had taken a body language class a couple of years ago, and he knew the crossed arms weren't good.

Or maybe they were. She looked playful and poised at the same time, and his blood ran a little hotter in his veins.

"Yes," he said simply. "Dinner at six. Program after that. You'd need a nice dress. I'm wearing a tuxedo."

"Is that so?" She grinned at him now, and Jeremiah kicked himself for not asking this woman out a year ago. "I have to check my schedule," she said. "Sometimes my weekends are insane with weddings."

"Ah, yes. Lots of weddings on the weekends."

"Right." She picked up her purse and took her coffee from the cup holder between them. He hurried to get out of the car with her, collecting the coffee for his employees from the backseat so he could walk with her. After all, she hadn't said yes yet.

Don't ask again, he told himself. *She said she'd check her schedule.*

"Anyway, let me know," he said when she got close to the glass doors leading into Your Tidal Forever.

"I will." She reached for the door handle. "Oh, wait." Jeremiah almost tripped over his feet he stopped so fast. "Yeah?"

"Maybe I should get your number, so I can text you if my Saturday is open." She looked at him with those glittering eyes, and Jeremiah thought he would've given her anything she asked for.

"Sure," he said, looking at the seven cups of coffee he held.

"Go ahead and say it," she said. "I'll text you, and then you'll have my number."

He recited it, and a moment later the device in his pocket buzzed. "I got it."

"Great." She watched him for another moment and then another, and then she cleared her throat and ducked into the building where she worked. It took every ounce of self-control Jeremiah had to keep walking to his own building, where he hit the handicapped button to get the doors open and himself inside with all that coffee.

He worked with six women, and yet he hadn't been able to get a date to the gala. He had female neighbors. A few lifelong friends that he could've asked. But he hadn't. He hadn't specifically been thinking about asking Shannon until he'd seen her crouched down in front of that flat tire.

And while she was crumpled and sweaty—the first time he'd ever seen her that way—she was the most beautiful woman in the world in that moment. And the idea to ask her to the gala had entered his mind before he'd even asked her for help.

"Morning, Flo," he said, setting the coffee on the counter in front of his receptionist. Three women worked behind the desk, keeping the files, making the appointments, and working with the insurance companies. He had a nurse who spoke to the kids before he did, and another therapist worked in the same office as him. Kelsie mostly did art therapy with the children as an additional step of their treatment. She had a nurse as well, and Sunny rounded out the six women Jeremiah worked with.

Honestly, he could use a little testosterone sometimes. To get that, he went to the gym before work and afterward too. He worked out with a trainer in the morning, and he simply ran in the evenings.

"Hercules is in your office," Flo said. "He was so sweet with my grandson last night."

"I'm glad." Jeremiah continued past the desk. "Did I beat Jerry in?"

"Tiffany's with him," she said. "He's been here maybe five minutes."

"And his mother didn't come in?"

"She's next door," Flo said as she shuffled some folders around. "She said her daughter is getting engaged soon, and she wanted to get some information."

"Hmm," Jeremiah said, adding the information to his

memory. Jerry was only eight, and he had five half-siblings from various relationships his mother had had over the years. She was not married to Jerry's father and never had been. He had no full blood siblings, and he struggled to fit in anywhere, which had caused him problems at home, school, and church—and ultimately, led him to Jeremiah's care.

He set the rest of the coffee on the desk down the hall where the others would get it and headed for his office. Upon opening the door, he expected to see a giant yellow lab waiting for him, and he wasn't disappointed.

"Hey, Herc," he said. "Did you have fun with Flo last night?"

The dog's tail started to thump the floor and Jeremiah ran his fingers down Hercules's back. "I asked Shannon out today. Can you believe it?" He collapsed into the chair behind his desk and sighed.

He pulled his phone out of his pocket and saw her text. *Thanks for the ride.*

He assigned her name to the text, and he stared at his phone, wishing and hoping she'd text to say she was completely free on Saturday night. She didn't, and he couldn't even pretend to know what she did for Hope Sorensen.

He did know Hope had been through four assistants in a year's time before Shannon had showed up. She was a bit intense and demanding, but Shannon had stayed and seemingly thrived at Your Tidal Forever.

Anytime, he tapped out and sent back. *And if you need a ride home tonight too, just let me know.*

She didn't text before Tiffany knocked on the door and said, "All right, Jerry. Go on in. Told you Hercules would be here."

The child entered and went straight to the lab, who sat there and let Jerry stroke him and play with his ears.

"How are you today?" Jeremiah asked without getting up. Most of his sessions were informal, and he just spoke to a child while they played with the dog or while they did homework.

"Fine," Jerry said.

"I didn't see your mom in the waiting room."

"She went somewhere," he said. "Said she'd be back before I was done."

"Tell me something good that happened this week," Jeremiah said, thinking that if he was in therapy, he'd be going on and on about Shannon Bell, whose number he now had in his phone.

———

WHEN HIS MIDDAY APPOINTMENT CANCELLED, JEREMIAH sat in his office, looking out the window at the building next to his. Your Tidal Forever. Shannon was in there somewhere, and she still hadn't answered him about a ride home. Or next Saturday.

His stomach growled, and he wanted to text her and

see if she had time for lunch. "She doesn't even have time to send a text," he muttered to himself, finally standing up. He wasn't going to text her again. He might be desperate to see her again, talk to her, smell that wonderful scent of her hair and skin, but he wasn't going to let her know.

He'd been hiding his crush for a year. He could do it one more day.

"Who wants to walk down to Manni's for tacos?" he asked the receptionists. "I'm buying."

"I'll go," Michelle said. "I think these two are having a phone war." She grinned at Flo and Janie, both women in their fifties. Sure enough, the phone rang, and Flo lunged for it at the same time Janie practically knocked the receiver off the cradle.

"Doctor Yeates' office," Janie said, a triumphant smile on her face. Flo rubbed her knuckles, which had taken some force from the phone as it skidded across Janie's desk.

"Okay," Jeremiah said brightly. "You and me, Michelle." She worked on filing and insurance payments, which was a huge headache, Jeremiah knew. She was also closer to his age, with a boyfriend who worked out at the cattle ranch several miles outside the main part of the city.

"Bring me back the tuna bites," Flo said. "And Janie will want the mahi mahi, since it's Monday."

"Monday special," Jeremiah confirmed. "Tuna bites." He and Michelle left the office, and though it was still March, the sun shone brightly over Getaway Bay. "So, how are things with Dan?"

Michelle sighed, which meant they weren't good. But Jeremiah said nothing. He didn't analyze his employees— or anyone else that wasn't paying him.

"He's going over to his mother's again."

"Well, she's been injured, hasn't she?"

"Oh, it was a pulled tendon in her foot," Michelle said, like that was something simple that didn't require any help.

"So we're not liking Dan."

"I just think he needs to cut the apron strings."

"I think it's the mother that usually does that," Jeremiah said, casting a quick glance to the front door of Your Tidal Forever as they walked by.

"Oh, I forgot to tell you," Michelle said, putting her hand on Jeremiah's arm. "A woman came by about an hour ago when you were with Max. She said she doesn't need a ride home, because she'll be…out somewhere?"

Jeremiah's heart beat out of control. "Was it Shannon?"

"Yeah, that's what she said her name was." Michelle smiled at him and tossed her long, sand-colored hair over her shoulders. "And they were going out to Petals and Leis to get flowers. I think."

"Okay," Jeremiah said, his pulse settling back to normal. He trudged down the boardwalk that would take them to Manni's and back, wondering when he'd be able to see Shannon again.

And why hadn't she just texted him that she didn't need a ride?

He frowned at the bluest sky in the world, thinking he probably better stuff his crush back into the box he'd been keeping it in for all these months.

Chapter Three

S hannon's stomach grumbled at her as she watched Jeremiah walk by with the blonde woman she'd spoken to earlier. She hadn't caught the woman's name, and the way she touched Jeremiah's arm suggested they might be together.

Her eyebrows pulled together. "Then why did he ask you to the recognition dinner next Saturday?"

And why hadn't she answered him yet?

"What?" Riley asked from a few feet away. Before Shannon could answer, Riley got up from her desk and approached the window where Shannon stood. She was waiting for Ash to finish up a dress consultation so they could go out to her husband's flower farm.

"Are you watching Doctor Yeates?" Riley's voice held entirely too much surprise.

"He asked me out this morning," Shannon said in a near-whisper.

Riley met her eye, and Shannon was so glad she had friends she could talk to about things like this. "And?"

Shannon quickly relayed what had gone on that morning, then she shrugged. "And I don't know. I haven't answered him, though next Saturday is open."

"Why not?" Riley demanded. "He's *gorgeous*, and he's a doctor."

"Yeah, a doctor who analyzes people. I don't need him...shrinking me up, you know?" Shannon wound her fingers around themselves. "So I don't know."

"You think he's going to ask you all kinds of questions?"

"He already did, on the short drive here."

"What kind of questions?"

"You know, siblings, if I grew up here."

"Oh, wow," Riley said, with mock horror in her voice. "*Definitely* don't go out with him. I mean, how dare he try to get to know you?" She giggled and quickly returned to her desk when a door opened.

Charlotte, Hope, and Ash came spilling out of Charlotte's office, along with a bride and her mother. Everyone was all smiles and white teeth, and Shannon stayed off to the side, out of the way. She had perfected blending in, only appearing at the exact moment Hope needed something.

"So we'll see you next month," Hope said. "Thanks for coming in."

The bride and her mother left, and Ash handed an armful of dresses to Shannon. "Ready?"

"Yep," she said.

"So you're going to source the flowers for the Bower event," Hope said.

"Right," Shannon said. "I'll text you pictures of everything, and we can get this done today."

"I'll keep my phone on." Hope turned back to Charlotte, and the two women went back into the office they'd just come out of.

Shannon turned to Riley, and said, "Bye, Rye. See you tomorrow."

"You're not coming back?"

"Not today," Shannon said. "Vivian Bower wants flowers on everything, and we have to select blooms for the trellises, the altar, the table settings, the wedding party." She looked at Ash. "It'll take hours, right?"

"At least," Ash said. "And we're stopping for lunch on the way, because I'm starving." She stepped over to the door and pushed through it, letting in some of the Hawaiian heat.

"Text me about the doctor," Riley said, shooting a look toward Charlotte's office, which still had the door open. Shannon watched it too, then she nodded and followed Ash outside.

"The doctor?" Ash asked almost as soon as the door had closed behind Shannon.

"How did you hear that?" she asked, sending a quick laugh into the air. "Riley practically whispered it."

"I hear everything," Ash said with a laugh of her own. "So tell me about this doctor."

And since Shannon didn't know what to do or how she felt, she laid it all out for Ash. She pulled into the parking lot at Petals & Leis with a "Wow, Shannon. You think too hard about stuff."

Shannon left the wedding dress samples in the back of Ash's car and joined her on the sidewalk. "I do?"

"Do you like this Jeremiah Yeates?"

"I don't even know him."

"But you've seen him around. You've spoken to him. He drove you to work today. Is he a nice guy? You could get to know him and not want to stab out your own eyeballs?"

Shannon chuckled and said, "Of course." He was a nice guy. Incredibly dressed. Tan and toned and totally datable.

"Then you better text him that you're available next Saturday, or he might ask that woman you saw him with on the boardwalk." Ash gave her an encouraging smile. "I mean, he has to have a date, right? He can't wait forever." She pulled open the door and went inside the building.

"Okay," Shannon said. "All right. I can text him."

Ash laughed. "It's a text, Shannon. It's not a boxing match." She paused and added, "Just don't say you're engaged when you're not. Trust me, that is not worth it."

Shannon barely heard her, but she nodded anyway. "Okay, can I have a minute?"

"Sure, I'll go say hello to Burke." Ash walked off in

pursuit of her husband, and Shannon stared at Jeremiah's messages on her phone.

It might not be a boxing match, but it certainly felt like one. Because Shannon hadn't been on a date—a real date—with a man in a very long time. Her schedule at Your Tidal Forever was insane, and she had the two cats, so she wasn't terribly lonely. And she honestly didn't know if she could trust a man again after what had happened with Richard.

Her nerves seemed to be firing cannons, and she couldn't get her thumbs to land on the right letters. She looked up and drew in a deep breath. "Come on, Shannon. You can do this. He isn't going to know about Richard, and you don't have to tell him."

The man was a doctor, yes. And yes, he was a child psychologist. But that didn't make him a mind-reader.

Saturday's wide open. She read over the text. Did it sound desperate? She quickly deleted it and tried again with, *I am available Saturday night. Let me know the when, where, what, and how, and I'll be there.*

Satisfied that her answer wasn't over-eager, she tapped on the button to send it to him.

Great, came back almost immediately. *Did you get your car figured out?*

She groaned when she realized she hadn't even had time to make a phone call since arriving at Your Tidal Forever. *No,* she tapped out. *Could I possibly get a ride to work in the morning?*

Before she could lose her nerve, she hit send. After

all, she had a number of girlfriends she could ask for a ride. She could call her father that evening and he'd let her borrow his car until hers was fixed. She could call a car service or take a taxi.

But there was a growing part of Shannon Bell that wanted to get to know more about Doctor Jeremiah Yeates. So she sent the text, hoping he'd say yes.

Of course, he said. *You tell me what time to leave so we get the good spot in line at Roasted.*

Shannon giggled, quickly glancing over her shoulder to see who'd heard. But there was no one there, and she allowed herself a moment to bask in the glow of seeing Jeremiah again.

Then she tapped out, *8:20 is the best time to show up at Roasted. So come get me at 8:10.*

With another opportunity to be with Jeremiah, Shannon turned with a smile on her face and a bounce in her step that hadn't been there before. Maybe this long afternoon of flower finding wouldn't be so bad now.

———

By THE TIME SHANNON KICKED OFF HER HEELS AND closed her front door behind her, a headache pounded behind her eyes. Jean Luc purred around her calves, and she gave the orange tabby a quick pat before heading into the kitchen for painkillers and something to drink.

Sure, she knew the orange soda she favored made her palette that of a ten-year-old, but she didn't care. She loved the smooth taste of a melted popsicle as the carbonation burned her throat.

After tossing back a handful of pills with several gulps of orange soda, she was feeling better already.

Good thing too, because within moments of her collapsing on the couch, someone banged on her door. Her father proceeded to enter the house with, "Shannon? You home?"

"Right here, Dad," she said, falling back to the couch cushions. She didn't need to get up to entertain her father.

"I have Roy taking the car over to Larkin's to get a new tire and a new spare."

Shannon managed a smile. "That's great, Dad. Thanks so much."

"You okay?" Her dad peered at her with knowing eyes.

"I've been home for about five minutes," she said. "And it was just a long day." Walking through flower fields should not happen in three-inch heels, but Shannon hadn't had any other footwear. She leaned back and closed her eyes. "I'm fine. I just need some dinner, and I'll be fine."

"I'll call Mom." As well-versed with technology as he was cars, her father called her mother and asked her to bring sushi.

"Not sushi," Shannon said. "If she's going to Sea Street, I want something from Mama Chu's."

Her dad related the message and hung up. "So,

which wedding are we working on now? I thought all of your high-profile shindigs were done."

"They are," Shannon said with a sigh. She opened her eyes to look at her dad. "All of the weddings at Your Tidal Forever are high-profile." At least it felt that way. Hope *wanted* it that way. She wanted every bride to feel like they were the gold standard, even if they chose the least expensive package.

"I'm not sure why you're still there," her dad said. "You could work for anyone on this island. Or open your own organizational consulting firm."

"I like working at Your Tidal Forever," she said. The job was tiring, yes. A bit stressful at times. But Shannon got paid well, and she loved all the people she worked with. She couldn't imagine leaving it for something else, striking out on her own or having to meet new people and make new friends.

Fear bubbled up in her bloodstream just thinking about it. So she put on a smile and said, "Do you want coffee?"

Her dad followed her into the kitchen, where she bustled around to make the brew and get out the flavored creamers she had. Then she went into her backyard and cut several lengths off her rose bush, replacing the old flowers on the island with the fresh ones.

She pulled out her plates and mugs, and by the time her mother walked in with the food, Shannon's headache was partially gone, and she hadn't had to answer any more questions about why she stayed at a job that did leave her physically and mentally exhausted most days.

But it was better than any alternative she could think of, and if her mind stayed busy, she didn't have to think about why she'd left her old job and gone to Your Tidal Forever in the first place.

The next morning, she felt like she had dozens of very hungry caterpillars eating their way through her insides. She couldn't believe she'd asked Jeremiah for a ride, even if he was handsome and available.

With new clarity this morning, she also wanted to cancel their date for next Saturday. No way she could go out with him. She couldn't believe she'd gotten in the car alone with him yesterday, and now she had to do it again?

She wrung her hands together as the clock clicked closer to eight-ten. She'd already fed her cats and made sure every little item was in its proper place, from her earrings to her sandals. She stood on the front porch, so she saw Jeremiah's car as it eased around the corner and continued toward her house.

"Go on," she told herself, especially when their eyes met and that crackle of attraction sparked within her. So maybe she could like this guy. Maybe he wouldn't turn out to be a creep. Maybe he'd be every bit the gentleman he seemed to be.

"Morning," she said as she moved down her front steps. Her voice sounded normal despite the caterpillars.

Jeremiah didn't get out of the convertible, but simply grinned at her and said, "Good morning, Shannon."

She got in the car and fastened her seatbelt, her huge bag at her feet. "Thanks for doing this. My car should be ready today."

"It's no problem," he said. "I literally live three blocks over." He glanced at her as he flipped the car in reverse and pulled out of her driveway.

"So I have one more favor," she said.

"Anything," he said, and then jerked his attention back to the road. His fingers tightened on the steering wheel, and Shannon wondered what was going through his head.

"Could you drive me over to Larkin's tonight to pick up my car?"

"Oh, sure," he said. "That's easy."

"Did you think it would be something hard?" she asked, surprised by the teasing quality of her voice.

Jeremiah chuckled. "Well, when a beautiful woman says she needs a favor, a man's mind can go in a lot of directions." He checked left and then right before pulling onto the main highway that would take them into downtown Getaway Bay.

Shannon's mind stalled on the word *beautiful*. She blinked a couple of times and said, "I think that was a compliment, Doctor."

"It was."

"Then thank you."

Without warning, he reached over and took her hand

in his. Shannon panicked, though his hand was warm and big and fit against hers just right. She pulled back, her heart racing. Her mind was desperately trying to catch her pulse, and she couldn't make sense of anything.

"I'm sorry," Jeremiah said, his voice soft and full of awkwardness. "I thought...." But he didn't finish, and Shannon didn't know what to say to explain her irrational behavior.

Chapter Four

Jeremiah had no idea what to do to fix things between him and Shannon. She'd been playful and flirtatious only moments ago. Why had he reached over to hold her hand?

Just because he saw his trainer, Brandon, do such a thing this morning didn't mean Jeremiah could do the same thing. Brandon was tall and built and worked out for a living. Every female who came into the fitness center looked his way, and as far as Jeremiah knew, Brandon went out with a lot of them.

But Jeremiah didn't need a lot of dates. He just wanted one with Shannon.

"We have to make a stop," he said.

"Oh?" she asked, and he was grateful she was able to speak.

"Yeah, I need to pick up my dog."

"Dog?" Her voice definitely held some alarm now.

"His name's Hercules, and he's the most gentle dog you'll ever meet. He's a therapy dog, for the kids." He glanced at Shannon and watched her physically relax. "Look, I'm sorry about that. I just thought we were getting along so well, and I really like you."

Horror struck Jeremiah, finally rendering him mute. Why had he said that? What was wrong with him this morning? Maybe his crush on this woman was too big to contain now that he'd opened the top flap of the box where he'd kept it all this time.

"It's okay," she said. "I have—I mean, my last boyfriend—"

Jeremiah heard panic and anxiety in every word she said, and he hated it. Wanted to erase it all. "It's really okay," he said.

"I don't want you to judge me," she said. "Or you know, try to get inside my head."

Jeremiah pulled into the driveway of Maribel Martin and put the car in park. "Is that what you think I'd do?"

Shannon lifted one shoulder in a small shrug, which meant yes, that was exactly what she thought.

"I have to go get Hercules." He suppressed a sigh as he got out of the car, and shock travelled through him when Shannon did too, meeting him at the front corner of the car.

"Look, I just have to tell you something," she said. "And—" Her mouth stayed open, but her voice muted as if someone had pressed a button.

She was jittery, and Jeremiah hated that his touch had

transformed her from the flirty fun woman he was crushing on hard to this scared shell of Shannon. He was extraordinarily good at waiting for people to talk, so he stuck his hands in his pockets, and did just that.

Shannon raised her chin, and Jeremiah made the mistake of looking right into her eyes. He lost himself for a time and he didn't even know how long.

"My last boyfriend," she started and that brought him back to the moment. She cleared her throat, but she did not look away from him. She possessed some serious strength and that only made her more attractive to Jeremiah.

"My last boyfriend assaulted me," she said, the last thing Jeremiah had been expecting.

His eyebrows went up, and then immediately down into a frown. "You mean…he…."

"He was my boss, and he tried to force himself on me."

Rage and fear struck Jeremiah right in the heart. "Shannon, I'm so sorry." He wanted to reach for her hand, hold her and tell her everything was all right. But it clearly wasn't. His brief touch had scared her, and he loathed that he'd done it.

"So I was just a little jumpy," she said. "In the car. I wasn't…expecting you to hold my hand."

"It won't happen again," he promised.

Shannon tilted her head, some of the anxiety bleeding out of her expression. "I just need, I don't know, maybe some warning next time."

Jeremiah lifted his eyebrows again, aware that Hercules had his nose pressed to the front window. The dog wouldn't bark; he was much too trained for that. But he'd clearly seen Jeremiah and wanted to come out. Now.

"Next time?" Jeremiah asked anyway, sure Hercules could give him a few more seconds.

"I mean, I wouldn't—" Her eyes flew to the door as it opened, and Jeremiah turned that way too.

"Hello, Maribel," he said, lifting his hand in a wave. "Be right in." The older woman hobbled out onto the porch, followed by Hercules, who came down the steps like the elderly canine he was. Jeremiah pointed at the ground, which told the dog to sit down at his feet. Hercules complied, which always made Jeremiah a little proud.

He faced Shannon again, but her attention was on Hercules. "Can I pet him?"

"Sure," Jeremiah said. "Herc, say hello."

Hercules hauled himself to his feet again and went closer to Shannon, who ran her hand along his head. The dog was in complete bliss, and his tail whipped back and forth to show it. Jeremiah chuckled as he tried to muscle his way between her knees.

"He has a sensitive spot right at the base of his tail," Jeremiah said. "Herc, knock it off. Come on. Let's get loaded up." He took a step toward the car, and Hercules came with him. He used to jump right up over the door into the back of the convertible with the top down, but now he waited for Jeremiah to open the door before he got in.

Jeremiah opened his door too, watching Shannon round the hood and go back to her side. They got in together, and he started toward the beachfront properties where they worked, his mind whirling and twirling with what she'd told him.

I mean, I wouldn't—

How would she finish that sentence? She wouldn't what? Ever want to hold his hand? Ever want him to think he had a shot with her?

But she'd said *next time* too, so Jeremiah didn't know what to think. He parked, got the dog out, and started down the sidewalk that led to the boardwalk that passed in front of his office.

"No coffee this morning?" Shannon asked, and Jeremiah froze.

"I forgot, with all the...with picking up Herc." He picked the dog up from someone almost every morning, and he'd never forgotten his coffee run at Roasted. No, he'd forgotten because of Shannon. The nearness of her addled his brain, and he couldn't make his thoughts line up.

He turned around. "I'll get yours too. The line's sure to be out the door by now." He took a few steps backward. "Maybe you can take Herc into your office with you? What do you get?" He'd seen her order caramel mochas before, but sometimes she got the Chai green tea, and sometimes the dark roast blend with extra cream.

She looked from him to the dog and back. "I'll just come with you," she said, and Jeremiah didn't want to argue with her. So he didn't.

They all loaded up in the car again, and this time, as soon as he'd turned onto the road that led back to the coffee shop, Shannon reached across the console between them and laced her fingers through his.

Surprise and joy twisted together and rose through him. He looked at her, and said, "So this is okay?"

"It's okay," she said. "Like I said, I just wasn't expecting it."

Jeremiah squeezed her hand, happier now than he'd been in a long, long time. "So you'll just tell me what's okay and when it's okay," he said. "Is that fair?"

"Is that okay with you?"

Jeremiah eased to a stop at the intersection and looked at her instead of checking both ways for oncoming traffic. "Shannon, of course it is." He did check for that traffic now, feeling some more word vomit coming up. "I've, uh, maybe had a little crush on you for a while. So yeah. You tell me what's okay, and when, and that'll all be fine with me."

"A little crush?" she echoed, pure delight in her voice now. "Is that so?"

"Yeah, that's so," he said, grinning at her and making the turn onto Main Street and heading down toward the other bay and Roasted. "Coffee's on me today. But none for you, Herc." He looked at the dog in his rear-view mirror and then cut a glance at Shannon. "The caffeine makes him cranky."

He was rewarded with the sound of Shannon's laughter, and it was more beautiful than he'd even imagined.

"Mom?" Jeremiah called that evening, having put in a long day at the office and not getting to drive Shannon home. Her car had indeed been fixed, and she'd caught a ride with a friend at work to the tire shop.

"In the kitchen," his mom called, and Jeremiah smelled the slightly burnt scent as he moved through the living room. He glanced around, but there was no evidence of anything scorched. No smoke.

"What're you making?" he asked, infusing a lighthearted note into his voice, still looking for that charred something-or-other—and now his father too. "Where's Dad?"

"Oh, he nearly burnt the house down making toast, so I sent him out to the garden. He's out there talking to the roses." His mother gave Jeremiah a smile. "And this is my homemade chicken noodle soup."

"You know it's almost summer, right, Ma?" Jeremiah smiled at her and pressed a kiss to her wrinkly cheek.

"Gertie is sick, so I'm taking most of it to her."

A lifelong neighbor, Gertie had been friends with Jeremiah's mother for probably fifty years. Maybe longer. Even he had a soft spot for the widow who'd crocheted him hats as a child, though he'd never needed one on the island.

"Should I see if she needs her lawn mowed tonight too?" he asked, already tired but determined not to show it. He let his dad putter around in the rose garden, but he'd forbid his parents from using any sort of power tool a couple of years ago. They both still had driver's licenses, but they didn't go to town much.

Jeremiah had turned them onto the grocery delivery service, and he stopped by several times a week too. There was an open invitation for them to ask for anything, and he'd bring it to them.

He came over every Tuesday night to get their lawn done, and he put their trash out before he left. He stopped by on Wednesdays to get the can back up the driveway and make sure they had everything they needed.

Truth was, Jeremiah loved his parents, and he didn't mind the huge time investment they required from him. After all, he didn't have much else going on in his life except his practice and his workouts.

"Her son is coming this weekend," his mom said. "So she's probably fine."

"All right," he said. "You and Dad are still coming to the dinner next weekend, right?"

"Of course," she said. "We wouldn't miss it."

Jeremiah nodded, wondering how to phrase his next sentence. "I got a date."

She didn't even turn from the stove, so the soup was

definitely more interesting than his love life. "Oh? Who did you ask?"

"This woman named Shannon Bell. She works in the building next to my office."

"Shannon Bell," his mother repeated. "That name sounds familiar."

"Does it?" Jeremiah didn't know much about Shannon's family, but she had said they'd lived on the island for decades. So maybe they knew his parents, though surely they were younger than his almost eighty-year-old mother and father.

"I don't know," his mom said. "Last night, your dad asked me what my grandmother's name was, and I couldn't remember it." She gave a light laugh, but Jeremiah knew his mother's memory loss bothered her. A lot.

"It was Susana," he said, giving her a quick kiss. "That's why you named Suzie, well, Suzie."

"Ah, yes," she said. "Susana Laura Blockly."

"Yep." Jeremiah gave her a quick smile. "Don't give away all of that soup. I'm going to go talk to Dad and get the lawn done. Then I want to eat."

"Okay," she called as he went out the back door, and Jeremiah got hit with the stunning beauty of Hawaii in his parents' backyard. From the lush trees, to the emerald green grass, to the brilliant blue sky.

Well, the sky was currently undergoing a gorgeous sunset, and the scent of flowers replaced the burnt-toast smell from inside. Sure enough, his father shuffled among the rose bushes that hadn't quite bloomed yet. But they would soon.

"Hey, Dad." Jeremiah lifted his hand in a wave and continued toward the shed in the back corner of the lot.

"Hey, Miah, come here for a second." Only his father called him Miah, and he actually liked it. He changed direction and paused on the threshold of the rose garden.

"Yeah?"

"Don't let your mother take that soup over to Gertie's," he said. "She twisted her knee this morning, and she's not stable enough to go down all our steps and up all of Gertie's."

"Twisted her knee? She didn't say anything about it."

"That's because she doesn't want you whisking her off to the hospital."

"Dad," Jeremiah said. "I had to take her last time. She needed stitches."

"I know, I know." He clipped something for a reason that escaped Jeremiah's intelligence. "But just volunteer to take the soup over."

"All right," he said. "Can I mow the lawn first?"

"Sure," he said. "There's plenty of time."

Jeremiah had learned that his parents did have plenty of time for anything they wanted now that they were retired. So he got the lawn mowed and his hands washed, and then he said, "Ma, I'll take that soup over on my way out."

"Oh, thank you, dear." The fact that she didn't argue indicated that she had indeed hurt herself.

He collected the jars of soup for Gertie and went down all the steps at his parents' place and up all the ones at Gertie's. After ringing the doorbell, he listened to the breeze blow down the street, almost imagining the roar of the waves as they crashed against the shore. But he knew he couldn't really hear them from here.

"Jeremiah?"

He turned at the familiar voice that was nowhere near old enough to be Gertie's. "Shannon?"

Chapter Five

S hannon stared at this new version of Jeremiah. A less refined man, without the suit and shiny shoes. He wore a ball cap, shorts, and a T-shirt, and he carried a bag with food in it.

"My mother made Gertie some chicken soup. I guess she isn't feeling well." Jeremiah held up the bag with a few jars in it.

Shannon simply stared at him. It seemed impossible that their paths had crossed so many times in the past and yet nothing had come of it. She glanced up and down the street. "Where did you come from?"

"Right next door," he said, nodding to his right. "My parents live right there." He extended the brown paper bag toward her and she took it.

"Oh, this is still warm," she said, the scent of yeast now meeting her nose. Freshly baked bread. It was one of Shannon's downfalls, and the main reason she had such curvy hips. "Come on in. Auntie is sleeping, but she'll be happy for the food when she wakes up."

"Gertie is your aunt?"

"Great aunt," she said. "She's my father's aunt." She followed him into the tiny, galley-style kitchen.

He set the jars on the countertop and faced her. "And you come visit her often?"

"Not that often, actually." She giggled, sucking the sound back in when she realized how girlish it sounded. "Tonight, I'd heard she was sick, and something told me to get over here and sit with her."

Jeremiah's blue eyes sparkled like sunlight glinting off the ocean. "Interesting." He edged closer to her, invading her personal space. Her initial reaction was to tense, to prepare to have to push him back.

But he just smiled and stepped past her. "Well, I won't stay long. I'm beat after today." He yawned, and it sounded a bit fake to Shannon.

She followed him back to the front door anyway, holding onto it with one hand while she tried to figure out what to do with the other. "Tell your mother thanks for the soup."

"I will." He watched her, his gaze so intent, Shannon wanted to close her eyes so she wouldn't have to keep looking into his. "See you tomorrow," he said, and took a step back. He turned and went down a few steps before twisting toward her again.

"Hey, Shannon?"

"Yeah?"

"Maybe we could go to lunch tomorrow."

And while the thought of lunch with him terrified her, Shannon found herself saying, "Sure, I'd like that."

He waved and went down the rest of the steps in front of her great aunt's house, leaving Shannon to wonder if she'd completely lost her mind. First she was holding hands with him—no, first she'd told him things she hadn't told anyone. Not even Riley or Charlotte. Besides her parents, no one knew about the things she'd suffered at Richard's hand.

She'd been kicking herself all day for what she'd told him and how she'd acted, but she obviously hadn't scared him off.

Yet, her mind whispered, and she worked to silence it. Jeremiah—Doctor Jeremiah Yeates—had a crush on her and had for a while now. She could like him. She could hold his hand. She was worthy of his attention.

And she really wanted some of that soup and bread too, so she went into the kitchen and served herself some. The negative self-talk disappeared, and Shannon sat in the living room while her great aunt slept down the hall. She allowed herself to entertain fantasies about Jeremiah, and the two of them falling madly in love and getting married.

Then she pulled back on the reins and grounded herself in reality. So he was handsome, kind, and employed. She'd held his hand once, and it was a long way from that to saying I do.

"So you'll start with lunch tomorrow," she said aloud to the house. Then she pulled out her phone and started texting Riley for the following day's schedule so she could make sure she had an hour in the middle of the day to see Jeremiah.

———

WHEN SHE ARRIVED AT YOUR TIDAL FOREVER THE following morning, Riley already sat at her desk. She stood so fast, the chair went flying into the wall behind her. "There you are," she said, a huge grin covering her face. "You're dating Jeremiah Yeates?"

Shannon glanced toward Charlotte's office and the hallway that led further into the building. "Shout it, why don't you?"

"Oh, I didn't shout it." Riley came around the desk. "I'm so happy for you, Shannon. You haven't been out with anyone in *ages*."

Shannon groaned and chose to ignore the underlying meaning behind Riley's words. "Don't remind me. I have no idea how to act on a date." She shook her hair back and gathered it into a ponytail. "And I'm not *dating* him. We're...friends."

"Friends?" Riley's voice pitched up terribly high.

"Yeah," Shannon said. "I mean, he asked me to go to his big recognition dinner next week, and we're going to lunch today, but that's not dating." Sudden fear struck her. "Is it?"

Riley grinned at her in the most wolfish way. "It sure is, Shannon."

"Well, we haven't even been to lunch yet," she said, walking toward the hallway that led down to her desk. "So technically, we haven't started dating yet."

"Mm hmm," Riley said, clearly not believing anything Shannon said. Which was fine. Shannon hardly believed herself. She put her purse in her bottom drawer and locked it, then settled in front of her laptop to pull up Hope's schedule for today.

She had a new bride consultation at eleven that she'd need the prep work for, and Shannon spun in her chair to pull it from the filing cabinet behind her. She put together every bride consultation folder, and she'd done this one last week.

Margaret Miller, who went by Maggie. She was marrying a man from the other side of the island, and their budget was small. But she wanted beach, and she wanted custom, and Shannon pulled a purple sticky note from the pad and wrote *Hillary* on it.

Hope wanted her recommendation for who to assign each bride to, and Hillary had just finished a wedding two weeks ago and had room in her schedule for another bride.

After placing that folder on the corner of her desk, she sorted through Hope's emails, flagging the ones that required her boss's attention. She answered any she could to keep them off Hope's plate, and she flat-out deleted others.

By the time Hope herself walked through the door, Shannon had her office open with a tray of individually wrapped fruit candies in a bowl, and the consultation folder on the round table where she met with potential new clients.

"The meeting with the city small business owners was moved to one-thirty," she said, placing a message about it on Hope's desk. "And Maggie and her sister Libby will be here in an hour." She nodded to the folder.

"Thank you, Shannon," Hope said, dropping her purse on her desk and looking at the message. "I'll get Aiden over to that meeting. His shoot was moved to this evening, as the bride wanted sunset photos for her announcement." She rolled her eyes and exhaled, as if the sunsets in Hawaii were too tacky for engagement announcements.

Shannon paused, waiting for her next assignment. Hope usually fired them off quickly, and Shannon had learned not to leave her office until she sat down.

"I'll need a report on those flowers from the other night," she said. "I want it broken down by cost in three options for Vivian."

"I've started on that and I'll have it to you by the end of today," Shannon said.

Hope gave her a grateful smile. "And we need to call The Lion House and make sure they have room in their catering schedule for our company party." She moved around to her chair, but didn't sit.

"Company party?" Shannon asked.

"Yes." Hope looked at her. "I've never done one, and I'd like to. I love all the people who work for me, and we need a way to recognize them, don't you think?"

"Sure," Shannon said.

"I'm thinking Fourth of July," Hope said, finally lowering herself into her seat. "Obviously not the day of, as people will be busy with their families, and we always seem to have a zillion weddings the first week of July. But sometime in there. Look at the calendar, would you? Find a date. Get The Lion House to cater it. Put together a plan for the celebration."

Shannon froze, her brain trying to catch up to her ears. "Me? You want *me* to put together a plan for the celebration?"

Hope smiled, and this time it was more motherly. "Yes, Shannon. You're the best assistant I've ever had, and I trust you. You know what I like."

Shannon did know what Hope liked. More importantly, she knew what Hope did *not* like.

"And besides," Hope said. "I won't be around forever, and Aiden and I don't have kids…." She turned and glanced out the window, looking at something Shannon could only imagine. She sighed and looked at her desk. "And we've worked so hard on this place, and I'd hate to just see it disappear."

Shannon took a couple of quick steps forward and

froze again. "And you think, I mean, you want...*me* to run it?"

Hope shrugged one shoulder, a knowing smile on her face. "You'd do a great job." She straightened, the moment clearly over. "But it's probably years away. I just think it would be nice to have someone to help out a little more." She turned to her computer, the conversation clearly over.

"I'll look at the calendar," Shannon said, nodding and getting out of the office as quickly as she could. Back at her desk, she collapsed into her chair, her mind spinning in a dozen different directions.

Hope wanted her to plan an event by herself. The company party—the first one Your Tidal Forever had ever done. During peak wedding season.

So venue, food, entertainment. All the moving parts moved through Shannon's mind, and she started typing them out into a to-do list on her laptop. She didn't want to overlook one single detail.

She answered Riley's call when Maggie arrived, and she clicked down the hall to meet the sandy-haired woman. She showed her and Libby to Hope's office, where her boss had absolutely everything ready and memorized.

She didn't normally take a lunch until much later, and Hope would be with Maggie and Libby for at least an hour. Shannon glanced at her desk, where her cell phone sat face-down. Could she call Jeremiah and see if he could go to lunch now?

Probably not, she thought, her hope deflating. Hope often buzzed out to Shannon's desk to ask for something, be it a pricing quote or a picture of one of their previous events or simply to get the bride-to-be a drink.

So she settled back at her desk and tapped out a quick message to him instead. *What time were you thinking you could go to lunch?*

Hope's schedule for the day was wide open after Maggie and Libby left, and surely Shannon would have an hour she could sneak away for tacos with the handsome doctor.

His text came back quickly and made her smile. *My last client finishes at one. Anytime after that, and I'm yours.*

I'm yours.

Shannon lifted her eyes from the words and stared at the wall across from her desk. Did she want Jeremiah Yeates to be hers? She'd liked the way his hand fit in hers. Liked the way he showed up at his parents' house to do their yard work and take their neighbor homemade chicken noodle soup.

She liked his easy-going demeanor and that he'd had a secret crush on her. She thought about how she'd seen him walking with that woman he worked with, and how she'd touched his arm, making a flare of jealousy come alive in Shannon's heart.

She definitely didn't want him going out with someone else, holding someone else's hand, or giving them flirtatious smiles in the line for coffee.

So yes, after several minutes of over-analyzing,

Shannon decided she wanted Doctor Jeremiah Yeates to be hers.

She wasn't sure how long she'd been thinking, but she startled when her phone buzzed and Hope asked, "Shannon, can you bring me the Robison wedding file, please?"

Chapter Six

The numbers on the clock had never moved so slowly. Jeremiah thought that surely God was playing a trick on him and actually making time go backward. Shannon had texted a couple of times, and they were planning to meet outside their buildings just after one.

Jeremiah was seriously considering taking the rest of the day off completely. He didn't have any kids coming in, though he did have paperwork and files to go over. So much paperwork. If he didn't come back and use the afternoon to get caught up, he'd pay for it later.

He honestly wasn't sure he cared. Lunch with Shannon was a more exciting prospect, and the day was perfect for surfing. Finally deciding, when he took Taylor's file back to Michelle, he said, "After Porter, I'm going to lunch and then I'll be gone the rest of the day."

Janey and Flo looked at him too, though there wasn't

much surprise in their eyes. "All right," Janey said at the same time as Michelle.

"What's my first appointment tomorrow?" he asked.

"Kelli at nine-thirty," Flo said without missing a beat. "And it's my birthday and you promised there would be cake." She smiled at him, and it warmed Jeremiah all the way through. He loved the ladies he worked with.

"Oh, there will be cake."

"Am I taking Hercules tonight?" Janey asked, and Jeremiah switched his attention to her.

"Can I take him instead?"

"Sure. I don't think my grandson can come tonight anyway."

"Great, thanks." Jeremiah didn't normally mind farming out Hercules to whoever needed him. But for some reason, Jeremiah felt like *he* needed the therapy dog that night. He knocked twice on the counter before turning and returning to his office. Five minutes later, he felt a year had passed. Tiffany knocked on the door and said, "Go on in, Porty."

The little blonde boy came in, his stuffed alligator clutched against his chest.

"Oh, you brought Allen," Jeremiah said, smiling at the child. "Did he want to see my newest trick?"

Porter nodded, his big blue eyes wide as Tiffany brought the door closed, leaving the doctor alone with his patient.

"All right." Jeremiah cleared his throat. "But I'm still

working on it, so you better tell him not to be upset if it doesn't work."

Porter glanced down at the alligator and whispered something to him. It had been Kelsie's idea to get the stuffed animal for Porter, who had a very difficult time talking to adults. He'd been in foster care for a year now, and his latest family seemed to really love him.

"Is he ready?" Jeremiah asked, smiling at the boy.

Porter nodded and Jeremiah opened the top drawer in his desk. "All right then. Come on over here. Make sure you can both see." He waited for the boy to come closer, and he adjusted his cards so the trick would work.

"Okay." He shuffled the cards, which were covered with blue patterns on one side and had cartoon characters and numbers on the other. He fanned them out. "Pick a card. Look at it real good. Show it to Allen."

Porter did as he was instructed, and Jeremiah swept the unchosen cards up and made a spot for Porter's card, quickly marking it as he put it in the pile.

"Okay, so sometimes we have to really watch what's going on around us," Jeremiah said. "And if we don't like it, we tell someone we trust." He switched his gaze to Allen. "Right, Allen? Who would you tell?" He cocked his head toward the stuffed animal and said, "Porter. Of course. I think I could've guessed that."

He flipped over a card. It wasn't Porter's. "Is this your card?"

"No," Porter said, and Jeremiah knew today was

going to be a good session. After all, Porter had just spoken to him and it had taken less than five minutes.

He flipped another card and immediately swept it off the desk. "That's not it either." He looked at Porter, who smiled. "Wait. Was that it?"

"No." Porter giggled, and Jeremiah wanted to scoop up the six-year-old and tell him he was going to be okay.

"Who would you tell if you saw something that made you upset?" he asked, still shuffling the cards. He took a peek at one, made a face, and tossed it away too. "Not that one."

"I'd tell you," Porter said. "Or my mom."

Jeremiah almost dropped the whole deck of cards. He caught himself and kept them moving. "All right. Let's see if I can get the right card this time." He flipped over five cards and asked, "Is it one of those?"

Porter's eyes rounded, and he nodded. "Yeah, it's there."

"Allen? Is he fibbing?" Jeremiah grinned at the alligator, and then he pointed to the mouse holding a pie with an eight-shaped candle in the middle of it. "It's this one."

"Yes." Porter looked from the card to him. "How'd you do that, Doctor Yeates?"

"It's magic, Porty. I can't tell you *how* I did it. It just... gets done." He swept all the cards back into a deck and put them back in the drawer. "Did you draw anything with Miss Kelsie last week?"

"No."

"Hmm. Well, what are we going to do today then?"

Jeremiah grinned at him. "I know. How about you tell me about your mom? That must be going good."

"She made me a birthday cake," he said.

"That's right," Jeremiah said, deciding to circle back to the fact that Porter had called Linda Lowry his mother when it had always been Linda in the past. "It was your birthday on Saturday." He pulled open another desk drawer and pulled out a box wrapped in blue paper. "Allen almost forgot to remind me last time, remember?"

Porter stared at the gift. "You got me something?"

"Yep." Jeremiah pushed the box closer to him. "But I want you to peek at it first, and don't let Allen see. He might not like it, and you'll need to decide what to do."

Porter took his hands off the stuffed alligator—something he rarely did—and reached for the box. The top lifted right off, and he tilted it at an angle so that Allen couldn't see in. Then he looked at Jeremiah again.

"Well?" Jeremiah asked. "What do you think?"

"I don't know," he said.

"They could be friends." Jeremiah leaned forward. "Like you and your mom are."

"My mom loves me," Porter said. "And she said if I wanted to, she and Daddy could adopt me."

"Is that right?" Jeremiah asked, happiness swelling inside him. "And what do you think of that?"

"I don't know," Porter said.

"Hmm." Jeremiah leaned away from the boy. "It sounds like you have some decisions to make." He nodded toward the box. "Sometimes those are easy, and sometimes they're hard."

"What should I do?" he asked.

"Oh, now that's like the magic trick. I can't tell you what to do. But remember how we talked about what we feel in our hearts?"

Porter nodded, pressing his lips together.

Jeremiah pulled open his drawer of tricks and retrieved a piece of gum for the kid. Porter snatched it up and started unwrapping it.

"And what does your heart tell you about...you know." He nodded to the box.

"I think Allen would like having a friend. I might could leave him at home if he had someone to play with."

Jeremiah nodded. "All right. I can see that. And your mom and dad?"

"I like them."

"You want to live with them forever? Have them be your family?"

Porter looked at Jeremiah for a long, long time. Finally he said, "My heart says yes."

"All right then. Why don't you take that new friend out and introduce him to Allen? I'll go get your mom." Jeremiah stood up as Porter took out the new stuffed animal—a frog about the same size as the alligator.

He made it to the door before he heard Porter say, "Allen, this is Fiona. She is so nice, and you guys are going to be great friends."

LATER, AS HE STOOD IN THE SUNSHINE AND WAITED FOR Shannon to exit the building, he thought he should probably listen to his heart a little more too. It had hurt for so long, he'd sort of forgotten how.

He thought of Elaine, and her long, dark hair, expecting the tightening of his muscles and the quick pulse. But they didn't come. He stood there, completely calm, and his heart told him he was over the woman that had broken them both so long ago.

"Hey," Shannon said, breaking into his thoughts.

He wondered how long she'd been there. "Hey." He grinned at her, the strangest desire to tuck her hair behind her ear raging through him. "The flower is pretty."

She instantly reached up to her hair, where a yellow orchid sat just above her ear. "Oh, thanks. I forgot I had that there." She started to remove it, and then tucked it in tighter.

He started down the sidewalk with, "Do we want to walk down the boardwalk a bit? Or drive somewhere?" He secretly hoped she'd want to drive somewhere, because it was *hot* outside.

"How much time do you have?" she asked.

"The rest of the day," he said. "I decided not to go back and do my paperwork. I just need to get Hercules when we're done."

"Oh, playing hooky."

He laughed, thrilled when she tucked her hand into his arm on the next step. "That's right. I think I'm going to go surfing."

"Mm, a surfing child psychologist. You know, I don't think those two things go together."

He enjoyed the teasing quality of her voice, glad he could flirt back with, "Well, if you play hooky too, you can come watch. Then you'll see that they absolutely go together."

She laughed now, and Jeremiah wanted to make her do that every day. "I can't skip this afternoon. I have a huge report to put together for my boss."

"What kind of report?" he asked, veering toward the parking lot.

"Remember how I went out to the flower farm a couple of days ago? She wants a cost analysis and three plans to present to the bride for next week."

Jeremiah chuckled and slid his hand down her arm, where he could lace his fingers through hers. A sigh passed through his whole body, and he reached into his pocket with his free hand to pull out his keys.

"I'm not sure what you just said," he said. "But it sounded really report-y."

She grinned at him. "I want to get a steak salad out at the Cattleman's Last Stop. What do you think about that?"

It was a twenty-minute drive there and twenty back. "I think that sounds amazing," he said, unlocking the convertible and opening the door for her. He tried not to notice the curve of her hip in that tight pencil skirt, but he did. And the waves in her hair. And the orange and lemon scent of her perfume.

He went around the back of the car to give himself five seconds to get his raging hormones under control, and when he got behind the wheel, he said, "You obviously eat red meat. What else do you like?"

"It's more a question of what I *don't* like," she said.

"Okay, start there."

"Well, I don't like tomatoes. And I don't like bees. I don't like people who are late, and I don't like snow."

"Snow?" he asked. "Have you actually ever seen snow?"

"We went to Utah for Christmas one year," she said. "My great uncle lives there. It is so cold, and yeah." She shuddered. "I don't like the snow."

"Good thing you live in Hawaii." He glanced at her out of the corner of his eye, and she was so carefree in his car. Her hair streamed behind her as he drove, and she gathered it into one hand and held it there.

"What about you?" she asked, catching him looking at her. "What are you going to order for lunch?

"Easy," he said, focusing on the road again. "Ribeye."

"And for Hercules?"

"I didn't bring Hercules."

"Yeah, but I saw you with him. You'll get him something."

Jeremiah took a moment to mull over her words. "Yeah, I probably will. He likes a good flank steak."

"Oh, so we get the good stuff for the dog."

"He's...." Jeremiah trailed off, because he knew what Hercules was to him, but he didn't know how to articulate it to this gorgeous woman. He swallowed and another mile went by, and still Shannon waited for him to finish his sentence. So he wasn't the only one with an astronomical wait time, and he searched for the words that wouldn't make him weak.

Chapter Seven

S hannon finally said, "You can tell me, you know," in a very quiet voice. So quiet she was sure Jeremiah wouldn't even be able to hear her.

"He's a therapy dog," he said, his fingers releasing and then tightening on the wheel. "And he didn't start with kids." He looked at her, and in that one moment when his eyes weren't on the road, she caught the vulnerability in his gaze. "He was for me."

Whatever Shannon had expected Jeremiah to say, that wasn't it. "Oh."

"I was engaged once," he said. "Her name was Elaine. I was hopelessly in love with her. When she called off the wedding...." He shrugged, leaving the words right there. "I maybe fell apart."

Shannon knew what *maybe fell apart* looked like. What it sounded like. What it felt like, way down deep in her soul.

"My father is a veterinarian, as well as an expert dog trainer. He used to train dogs for agility courses, and he knew a lot of people who trained dogs for all kinds of things. He got Hercules for me, and well." Jeremiah swallowed again, and Shannon was beginning to see that nervous swallow was his tell of anxiety.

"I saw someone for a few months, and Hercules would alert when I had panic attacks."

"How did he do that?" she asked, genuinely wanting to know.

"He'd lay right on top of me," Jeremiah said. "If I was in bed and couldn't get myself out." His voice took on a haunted quality. "If I was sitting, he'd come over and lean right into me, calming me down enough to pat him. Petting a dog is very therapeutic."

She nodded, her eyes focused out the windshield now. "How did he know?"

"He'd been trained to know," Jeremiah said. "Like I showed this kid a card trick today. Hercules is like that. He could sense something inside me, and he'd come press his head right into my chest, demanding attention from me, and I'd calm down."

"And now he works with kids." Shannon wondered if he could work some magic on her, but she was afraid to ask. Afraid to admit that she might still be broken, way down deep inside.

"He'll go wherever he's needed," he said. "Sometimes Flo—she's my receptionist—takes him home with her. Since her husband died, she doesn't like being alone at night. Her grandkids love Herc."

"And Maribel. Was that her name?" Shannon looked at Jeremiah now, almost craving the opportunity to look into his bright, blue eyes.

"Yeah, Maribel. She has some anxiety about her son being in the military," he said. "So Hercules goes over there from time to time."

"And you don't need him anymore."

Jeremiah exhaled, glanced toward the ocean, and looked at her, rewarding her with those beautiful eyes. "I still need him from time to time, Shannon," he said. "But I'm willing to share him too."

The Cattleman's Last Stop came into view, and she focused on it, the question she wanted to ask stuck somewhere behind her ribs. Jeremiah pulled into the gravel parking lot and swung his car into an empty space. It wasn't the normal lunch spot on the island, and in fact, it looked like they might have the whole place to themselves.

"Look," he said, finally releasing the wheel. "Elaine was six years ago. I'm not still hung up on her."

"Okay."

"I can tell you have something you want to say," he said. "So just say it. But I promise I'm not still dealing with feelings for Elaine."

"It's not that," she said, a blast of anxiety hitting her. In that moment, she wondered what Hercules would do, and she was very glad he wasn't there with them.

"Then what?" he asked, searching her face.

She tried to hold the words back. Even pressed her lips together. But she couldn't win against this tide. "Would you be willing to share Hercules with me?"

A figurative light bulb went off above Jeremiah's head, and Shannon saw the understanding roll across his face. He reached over, hesitated, and then tucked her hair behind her ear. She couldn't help leaning into his touch, stealing the comfort from his warm hands, his nearness.

"Of course I'll share him with you," he said. "You want to take him tonight? I was going to have him, but—"

"No, I don't need him tonight," she said, though she really did want that big, yellow lab with her in her big, empty house.

Jeremiah cocked his head, apparently hearing more than what she'd said. Then he practically leapt from the car. "Should we go eat? I'm suddenly starving."

Shannon wondered what had lit a fire under him, and she got out of the convertible a little slower. He extended his hand toward her, an open invitation for her to take it, which she did. As they walked up the wooden ramp to the front door, he pressed his lips to her forehead, and said, "You can have Herc whenever you want him, sweetheart. Just say so, okay?"

She paused and looked at him. "Okay, but tonight, I think he should stay with you."

Jeremiah nodded, reached for the doorknob, and let

her go first into the restaurant. It was easily the best meal of her life, with a funny, witty man who knew how to carry a conversation. They talked about light things, from their families to their favorite traditions on Getaway Bay.

"I love the family beach picnic," he said.

"And see, for me, it's always Santa's sleigh being pulled by the dolphins." She grinned and waved away the waiter when he asked her if she wanted more soda. Her stomach would probably be hurting for the rest of the day with the two glasses she'd already consumed.

Jeremiah drove them back to the office, the wind through her hair welcome, and the atmosphere between them easy and casual. Shannon felt the best she had in years, and she couldn't help smiling to herself as the beach rolled by.

"So I'll see you tomorrow," he said, fiddling with his car keys as they approached the turnoff in the sidewalk that would take her back to Your Tidal Forever.

She paused and looked up at him. "Yeah, about eight-ten." She tucked her hair, very aware of the last time Jeremiah had done it, but she couldn't get herself to walk away. She finally turned toward him, searching for the bravery she used to have.

"Lunch was great," she said, putting one hand on his shoulder and tipping up onto her toes so she could press her lips to his cheek. "Thank you so much for taking me. I don't get out of the office as much as I should."

Her phone buzzed in her purse, but she ignored it.

Jeremiah smiled down at her. "Maybe we could get together tonight too. I mean, I'll have Hercules, and maybe we could just, I don't know, go for a walk."

Shannon wanted to see him again, so she nodded, and that got her feet moving toward the doors of Your Tidal Forever. A warm glow enveloped her, almost like someone had poured hot honey in her veins. She turned back at the door to find him still standing on the boardwalk, his hands casually in his pockets.

She lifted her hand in a flirty wave and ducked inside. She knew the moment she took a breath inside the building that something was wrong.

Number one, Riley wasn't sitting at her desk.

Number two, the faint sounds of crying could be heard.

Number three, her phone buzzed again.

Number four, Hope yelled, "Shannon! Does anyone know where Shannon is?" from down the hall.

She didn't bother to check her phone, choosing instead to run down the hall toward Hope. What had happened? Was it the Newton flowers, because she had ordered those correctly. There would still be time to get them, though, because the wedding wasn't for another six weeks. Maybe something had happened with Vivian....

"I'm right here," she said, coming to a stop when she saw the bubbles.

Suds—so many suds—churned out of the dishwasher in the small kitchen at the back of the building. Hope herself was covered from neck to torso in them, and then up to her knee.

"What in the world?" she asked, wondering why she needed to solve a dishwasher emergency. The thoughts that had been tumbling through her head about which wedding had been affected disappeared, and she started laughing.

Riley wiped her hair out of her face, but she only succeeded in smearing soapy suds along her forehead. "There's Shannon," she said weakly.

Hope looked at Shannon and said, "I think I put the wrong soap in the dishwasher," only two seconds before she started to slip.

Shannon lunged toward her, but there was no way she was faster than gravity. Hope went down, and Shannon lost sight of her as she disappeared beneath the waves of bubbles still oozing across the floor.

And she couldn't help it—she started laughing. "I'm sorry," she said between chuckles. "I am. Give me your hand, Hope. Come on."

By the time she got home, her feet ached and she couldn't wait to get out of the wrong-sized clothes she'd borrowed from Hillary. She'd driven through a fast food restaurant for a fried chicken sandwich, and she sat on her front steps to eat it. If she went inside, then Jean Luc and Fuzzy would want some of her dinner, and Shannon was starving.

She'd texted Jeremiah about the dishwasher incident, and all about how long it had taken to clean up. He hadn't answered for the longest time, and then he'd commiserated with her for the last fifteen minutes of her day.

Her phone buzzed again, and she almost threw it into the nearest flowerbed—which would need to be weeded and planted that weekend. Shannon sighed. Maybe she'd come far enough in her career to hire a gardener. Hope had practically said that Shannon would get to run Your Tidal Forever should Hope want to retire.

Glancing at her phone over her chicken sandwich, she learned that Jeremiah was on his way home from the beach and wanted to know if she needed dinner.

With her pinky finger, she tapped out a *Nope. Eating now* and sent him the message.

Okay, he said. *Well, I have to go see my parents, so we'll have to raincheck that walk.*

Shannon actually breathed another sigh of relief at that. She really just wanted to eat, get out of these clothes and shoes, and soak in a hot bath.

She'd already kissed Jeremiah today, and maybe they needed some distance to make sure the relationship was right.

Shannon did, at least. She felt like she was on a roller coaster—up one moment and swooping down the next. She didn't trust herself to know how she was feeling in the moment, so she may have acted spontaneously or irresponsibly when she'd kissed him that afternoon.

She groaned, finished off her sandwich, and went inside where both of her cats sat a few feet from the door. Neither of them looked pleased, almost like they knew she'd considered bringing a dog home and that she'd eaten on the porch so she wouldn't have to share with them.

"Hey, guys," she said brightly. Fuzzy came forward and wound between Shannon's ankles, but Jean Luc just looked at her with that aloof expression on his face. "Good to see you too," she called after him, wondering what was more ridiculous—kissing Jeremiah or talking to a cat.

Chapter Eight

Jeremiah loved surfing. The sand. The waves. The way Hercules bounded through them like a dog half his age.

But he did not like the sand and how it got into absolutely everything. Every inch of skin seemed coated with it, and he really just wanted a shower. But after he'd texted Shannon about dinner, his mother had called him to say that his dad needed him for an hour and could he possibly come.

Jeremiah could, of course. Jeremiah always had in the past.

Suzie, his sister, was great about helping out too, but she'd landed a new gig in a luau that had her practicing with fire most nights. So Jeremiah had picked up the slack, and he went down Main Street toward the opposite end of town from the Sweet Breeze Resort and Spa.

When he pulled into his childhood driveway, he ran his hand through his crusty hair, hoping his dad just needed help getting a lid off a jar of pickles or something. He climbed the steps, glad he'd taken the afternoon off from work to spend time in the ocean. The waves always rejuvenated him at the same time they took physical energy from him.

"Come on, Herc," he said to the dog still laboring up the steps. Once Hercules stood beside him, he opened the front door and called, "Mom!" only moments before a chorus of people yelled, "Surprise!"

Jeremiah's heartbeat bounced in his chest, and he stared around at the familiar faces gathered in his parents' house. Flo, Janey, Michelle, of course. Kelsie and Tiffany and Sunny too. Several neighbors from up and down this old street, as well as a couple of Jeremiah's friends from surfing and the gym. Even his trainer, Brandon, was there.

In the middle of them all, his mother stood holding a cake, beaming at him like it was his birthday.

But it wasn't his birthday.

"What's going on?" he asked, glancing from person to person, glad they were all here but missing the one beautiful face he wanted to see. "It's not my birthday."

"The news that you're the recipient of the Getaway Bay Professional Dignitary Award was announced today," his mother said.

"Didn't you know?" his dad asked. He turned to Cal

Gallivan, a neighbor to the north. "How could he not know?"

"Look at him," Cal practically yelled, setting off a couple of other neighbors. "He looks like he's been rolled in sand."

Jeremiah had, in fact, been rolled in sand.

"Yeah, he's all wet," someone said, though that wasn't true.

"Look at that dog. Juliet, that dog is going to ruin your carpet."

"Did someone say there was cake?"

Jeremiah grinned at the elderly people in the living room, one hand absently reaching for Hercules, who was also a bit sandy.

Suzie came forward and wrapped him in a hug, giggling. "Congratulations, Doctor Yeates. Come eat some cake." She turned back to the crowd and said, "It's time for cake!"

If possible, that announcement only made everyone talk louder, and the crowd moved through the small kitchen and into the backyard. Jeremiah was one of the last people out there, and he marveled at the tables and chairs that had been set up in the yard.

"This must've taken them hours," he said.

"Oh, I brought over a couple of divers," Suzie said. "They had it done in like, ten minutes." She laughed again and moved away. Jeremiah watched her go, smiling and talking to everyone. She was so positive and so vibrant, and yet she couldn't find anyone to settle down with either. Suzie at least dated, and Jeremiah once again thought of Shannon.

Of course, he hadn't told anyone about Shannon yet, savoring the secret of her and the way she'd kissed him that afternoon for himself. He thought about texting her, but he didn't want to make a big deal out of her presence at the party, and it would certainly be a huge event to have her show up late. There would be introductions that had to be made, and the party would probably be over by then anyway.

So he smiled and accepted everyone's congratulations. He wished he'd gone home to shower first, but no one seemed to mind that he was crusted with salt and sand—or at least they didn't say it again.

He consumed cake and talked to his trainer about how they'd work it off in the morning. His father read the announcement of the Dignitary Award off of Suzie's phone, and everyone clapped.

Jeremiah accepted their kindness with as much grace as he could muster, but after about thirty minutes, he wanted to take his dog and get on home.

By the time that happened, though, the sun was almost dipped completely into the ocean and Hercules could barely move. "Come on, bud," Jeremiah said as they walked down the steps to the car. "You can do it. Come on."

He helped the elderly dog into the convertible and drove them both home. Jeremiah usually worked in his office or watched TV, but tonight, he stepped straight into the shower and then collapsed into bed after hefting Hercules onto the mattress next to him.

They both slept like the dead, and Jeremiah woke with visions of coffee and a certain dark-haired beauty in his mind.

He didn't see Shannon at Roasted on his way into work, and he had a full day of clients ahead of him. Not to mention all that paperwork he'd skipped out on the day before. By the time he got back to his phone, it had blown up with texts.

The news about the Dignitary Award had really hit town, and everyone he'd ever interacted with even a little bit had texted to say congratulations.

Shannon was one of them, and he frowned at the informal text from her. Besides, she already knew about the nomination for the award and had already told him congratulations.

He stared at his device, trying to figure out how he felt and what he should say in return. Before he could do anything, Tiffany knocked and his next patient walked in.

Jeremiah put his phone in his top drawer and locked it. After all, Jake had a bit of a tendency to steal things that didn't belong to him. The teenager was improving though, and Jeremiah simply held out his hand, and Jake put his phone in Jeremiah's palm without argument. That in itself was a huge win that had taken months to accomplish.

"So you're in the surfing competition," Jeremiah said.

"How'd you know that?"

"I read the local news," he said. "And I've been known to catch a wave or two."

Jake looked aghast, like someone Jeremiah's age would surely be unable to get up on a surfboard. He blinked and said, "It's in a couple of months. I'll probably lose."

"Tell me why you think that," Jeremiah said, another session underway.

―――――

WHEN HE FINALLY LEFT THE OFFICE THAT NIGHT, THE SUN was once again nearly down. It was still light enough that he could see the woman sitting on the hood of his car, and Hercules lowered his head and gave a low growl in the back of his throat.

"It's Shannon," Jeremiah said to the dog, and wow, his heart suddenly tap-danced through his chest.

"Hey," she said when he was several paces away. "Busy day?"

"Yeah," he said, not quite sure where they stood. Her text from earlier had felt so...odd, and he'd never responded to it. "Six clients, and all this paperwork." He sighed. "Sometimes I question my life choices, you know?"

She shook her head, a smile on her face. "I don't believe that."

"No?" He didn't move any closer to her, though almost everything in his body wanted him to.

"You wouldn't be getting this big island award if you weren't really good at what you do."

"Just because you're good at something doesn't mean you love it," he said.

Shannon slid off the front of his car. "What's going on?"

Jeremiah shrugged, half of him rejoicing as she moved closer and the other half wanting to step back. Give himself more room. Keep breathing air that wasn't filled with the sweet scent of her skin.

He was so confused, and he finally blurted, "I'm just going to be honest. I'm getting some mixed signals."

Her hand, which she'd started to reach toward him, fell back to her side. "Yeah, I suppose you are."

"So it's not just me?" he asked. "I mean, you're flinching away when I touch you, and then holding my hand, and then kissing me...." His voice died, and he watched her, wishing there was more than the orange street light to illuminate her face.

"I feel a little all over the place," she said. "I'm not trying to, you know, lead you on, or send you mixed signals."

Jeremiah nodded. "I know that." But he still felt like he wasn't sure how he felt, or how she did. *She* didn't know how she felt.

"Have you eaten?" she asked.

"No."

"Maybe we can just grab some dinner, and I don't know. Talk."

"You want to go out?" Jeremiah hoped she'd say no.

"If you want."

"I don't want to," he said, deciding to be honest. "I'd love to get some food and find somewhere quiet to eat. A park. My place. Somewhere away from the crowds." He thought of his phone and how many texts he'd gotten that day. He'd seen his picture online, and he didn't feel much like being a celebrity that night.

Hercules laid down, leaning into Jeremiah's leg. He leaned down and gave the dog a couple of good pats on the side of his chest. "Hercules likes this park out by the lava fields. It'll be dark, but it'll be quiet."

"Sounds great."

"Where do you want to eat?" he asked, taking a step closer. Since she'd told him about the assault with her ex-boyfriend, Jeremiah hadn't initiated much touching between them. He wasn't sure when it was okay to touch her and when it wasn't. He'd tucked her hair earlier and she'd barely blinked.

His eyes dropped to her mouth, but he wasn't stupid. He knew it was much too early to kiss her, and instead, he reached for her hand. "Chinese food?"

"Easy to eat without a table," she said.

"Let's hit Kimmy Sim's," he said. "They have the best wontons on the island."

"I can safely say I've never eaten there."

"You're really missing out then," Jeremiah said, squeezing her hand. "You want me to drive?"

"Yes," she said, and he felt a measure of vulnerability from her.

"All right. Come on, Herc."

The dog was able to get into the car himself, and he seemed as equally obsessed with Shannon as Jeremiah was, because he kept sticking his head between them like he'd try to climb into her lap.

"Lay down," Jeremiah finally said, glad when the yellow lab obeyed. They got their Chinese food and he drove ten under the speed limit out of the downtown area and around the island toward the lava fields.

A weak streetlight lit the park's entrance, and he turned off the main road and continued a little further.

"We used to come here as kids," Shannon said. "My dad loved to go fishing, and my mom would get so bored. So she'd walk up here and explore on the black rocks."

"They've redone the parking lot," he said. "Put in some benches and bathrooms." He pulled up to the only building, where the bathrooms were. Though it was dark, the ground out here held plenty of heat, and he got off the asphalt as quickly as he could. A small patch of grass surrounded the bathrooms, and Hercules settled at the end of the bench, knowing he'd get something from one of the bags of food eventually.

He passed out the food, asking Shannon what she wanted and giving her the plastic utensils.

"Are you happy about the award?" she asked, forking up a bite of food and putting it in her mouth.

"Yeah, of course," Jeremiah said. "I just don't like all of the attention."

She nudged him with her elbow. "Even from me?"

Jeremiah smiled into the darkness and picked up another wonton. "Yeah, well, I like the attention from you. Happy now?"

Chapter Nine

Shannon was very happy now. The food was excellent, and she wondered why she didn't go to Kimmy Sim's more often. Probably because it was out of the way and more expensive than the other places on the island.

Jeremiah didn't say a whole lot, and that was okay with Shannon. Hercules moved to her feet and laid right on them, which made her feel comfortable.

"You want to take him home with you tonight?" Jeremiah asked.

"Oh, I don't know," she said. "I have two cats."

"Two cats?" Jeremiah chuckled. "Hercules is practically perfect, so he'll probably be fine."

"Jean Luc is quite snooty," Shannon said. "But Fuzzy is nice."

"Jean Luc?" Jeremiah laughed fully now, and Shannon joined in.

"Yeah, well, my father loved *Star Trek*, and maybe I picked up a few names."

Twenty minutes later, Shannon walked up the front steps to her door, Jeremiah half a step behind her. "Sorry I'm not great company tonight," he said.

"You were perfect company tonight." She turned to face him. "Sorry I'm not really sure how I'm feeling and…." She didn't know how to finish, so she didn't.

"It's okay," he said. "Want me to stick around to make sure Hercules doesn't eat your cats?"

"Will he do that?" Shannon glanced down at the dog. She couldn't imagine him ever doing anything harsher than yawning.

"No," Jeremiah said with a scoff. "But I better come in and make sure anyway." He wore a sparkle in his blue eyes, and Shannon shook her head.

"Okay, but I haven't been home all day, so don't judge." She opened the door, a tremor of trepidation flowing through her. Fuzzy and Jean Luc waited a few feet inside the door like they always did, but as Hercules entered the house alongside her, Jean Luc hunkered down, hissed, and streaked away. Fuzzy stayed for a moment, and then she followed Jean Luc without the hiss.

"So I think it's safe to say the cats will stay hidden," she said, realizing Jeremiah had entered the house and closed the door behind him.

"Shannon, your place is great," he said, glancing

around. "Look, you have fresh flowers on the counter." He beamed at them and then her. "This place is exactly you."

Shannon wasn't sure what that meant, but she did like her house. "I painted the walls myself," she said, walking into the kitchen with Hercules at her side. "And my mother made the curtains in here." Nerves ran through her, and she couldn't believe she was talking about the window dressings—which she actually wanted to replace.

"Do you want something to drink?" she asked.

"No, I'm going to take off." Jeremiah put his hand in hers and smiled. He was calm while she felt like a tornado had torn through her chest. "Okay? I'll see you later." He fell back a few steps and added, "See you tomorrow, Herc."

Shannon watched him turn and walk back out the front door, and she moved to the couch and sank onto it. "What am I doing?" she asked Hercules, who once again came over to her, sat, and leaned into her. She scratched his head and ran both hands down the sides of his face.

And Jeremiah was right. The simple act of patting Hercules calmed her down. "I sure like him," she told the dog. "But I have no idea what I'm doing, and I'm...scared."

She was so, so scared, and she didn't know how to see past it to what might be on the other side.

"One step at a time," she whispered the advice which

her therapist had given her years ago, after the incident with Richard. She'd told Shannon she didn't have to fix everything in one day, or even one month. All she had to do was take one step at a time.

————

"NOT TOO FAR, MICHAEL," CHERYL CALLED TOWARD HER son. Shannon sat next to her sister under the umbrella, the sound of the surf and the smell of the sea like old friends. Her sister turned to her. "I swear, he has selective hearing."

"He's five," Shannon said, like that explained every-thing. And it usually did. Right where the water met the land, Cheryl's husband Bastian played with their daugh-ter. Also a five-year-old McKayla didn't seem to have the same risk-taking DNA as her twin.

Shannon adored her niece and nephew, and Cheryl was pretty great too. A few years younger than Shannon, she'd taken Shannon to her first therapy appointments and sat with her while Shannon talked to her parents about Richard.

"So I have some interesting news," she said, posi-tioning her sunglasses to make sure Cheryl wouldn't be able to see her eyes.

"Yeah? Another prince tying the knot on the beach?"

"No, thank goodness." Shannon sighed. While neither the bride nor groom had been all that particular about the details of the wedding, Noah Wales *was* a prince, and his entire royal family had attended the wedding. "And that was in a backyard," Shannon added.

"Oh, of course."

Shannon didn't have to look at her sister to see her rolling her eyes. Cheryl had a way of rolling her whole head when she found something ridiculous.

"So what's the news?" Cheryl asked.

Shannon took her time stretching out, just letting her bare feet out of the shade and into the sun. She loved lazy Sundays like this, and she wondered if she and Jeremiah would come to the beach on the weekends. Pack a cooler and bring the kids and just let the hours roll by one at a time.

"I'm seeing someone," Shannon said, a touch of glee in her voice.

Cheryl choked, and she started coughing. "Warning," she said, still choking. She got herself under control and stared at Shannon, who refused to look at her sister. "I need more warning next time."

"I warned you," Shannon said, folding her arms. "I said I had interesting news."

"I thought you were going to say some celebrity had come into the shop or something."

"Because that's always my news," Shannon said, anger tripping through her. Maybe not anger, but definitely annoyance.

"No," Cheryl said quickly.

"Yes," Shannon argued. "Is it so hard to believe I can get a date?"

"Of course not, honey." Cheryl put her fingertips on Shannon's arm, which utterly deflated her. "It's just that…since…you know. You *haven't* dated."

"I know. I think maybe it's time to move on."

Cheyenne arrived, kicking sand and exclaiming, "Why are you so far down? I had to walk like a mile to get here." She huffed and puffed, causing her two older sisters to look up at her.

"I have to keep an eye on Michael," Cheryl said. "And besides, it's not that far down."

Cheyenne set up her beach chair and flopped into it. "What a day."

"Sell a million houses this week?" Shannon asked.

"Just two," Cheyenne said, her sense of humor and hyperbole not the greatest.

"Shannon has a boyfriend," Cheryl said, and Cheyenne fell out of her chair. Literally. Fell right out onto the sand.

"What?" she asked, her arms splayed to her sides.

"Oh, come *on*," Shannon said. "It's so surprising that you fell out of your chair?" She shook her head, her bliss at this lazy Sunday afternoon at the beach completely gone now.

"She's moving on," Cheryl said.

"I was adjusting myself and the chair folded a little." Cheyenne stood up and brushed sand from her body before pulling her chair out farther and sitting again. "That's great, Shan. Who is it?"

"I'm not telling."

"Come on," Cheryl said. "That's not fair."

"You choked," Shannon said, pointing a finger at her next youngest sister. "And she fell out of her chair." She hooked her thumb at Cheyenne. "I don't need this in my life."

Only the wind whispered between them, and then Cheryl started giggling.

"Stop it," Shannon said, but the fight had already left her body.

Cheyenne laughed too, and before Shannon knew it, she was cackling with her sisters too.

"Fine," she said, trying to sober up. "Fine. I'll tell you. But you have to promise not to put any pressure on me. We're...it's new, and it's been going okay, and I'm hopeful."

"How new?" Cheryl asked.

"Uh, I guess it's been almost a week. He asked me out last Monday after I got my flat tire at the coffee shop." Shannon couldn't believe it had been almost a week since then. It had felt longer, and she wondered how time had a way of playing with her mind. She'd seen Jeremiah every day since then, even yesterday when they went to the farmer's market out at the cattle ranch.

"Okay, no pressure promise," Cheyenne said. "Cheryl?"

"No pressure."

Shannon looked at one sister then the next. "It's Jeremiah Yeates."

"The doctor?" Cheyenne practically screeched.

"The guy getting Getaway Bay's biggest award?" Cheryl asked, her voice made of pure incredulity.

And if Shannon hadn't already felt like Jeremiah was way out of her league, she certainly did then. She pressed her lips together, tightened her arms across her chest, and gave a single nod.

"He's gorgeous," Cheyenne said next.

"How'd you meet him?" Cheryl asked.

Shannon seriously didn't want to answer any more questions. She loved her sisters, and she probably should've been able to predict their reactions.

"He's too good for me," she said, all her old insecurities and fears rearing up inside her like a tsunami. "I'll break up with him."

But she couldn't do that before the event on Saturday night. Could she?

"You don't need to break up with him," Cheryl said. "He's definitely not good enough for you."

Shannon rolled her eyes. "Don't make yourself a liar, Cheryl."

Her sister sighed with a touch of frustration in the sound, but Shannon felt the same way.

"I didn't mean to make you feel like you weren't good enough for him," Cheryl said.

"Yeah, of course you are," Cheyenne added. "And

hey, you got a date. I haven't been on one of those in months."

Shannon softened, especially when Cheryl reached over and took her hand. "So, how'd you meet him? How many times have you gone out? Tell us about him."

Shannon looked at her then, and she saw genuine concern and compassion in her sister's eyes. Tears welled up in Shannon's eyes, and her throat narrowed. "Sorry," she said. "I just...things are hard. Dating is hard work, and I'm a little nervous about it."

"Of course you are," Cheryl said.

"But you don't need to be," Cheyenne said. They'd probably rehearsed this tag team speech for when Shannon started dating again. But she didn't mind. "If he's a good one, he'll understand."

"I told him about Richard already," Shannon said.

She saw the surprise lift Cheryl's eyebrows, but her sister put them right back down. "Seriously, Shan. Start talking. We want all the details."

Shannon watched the waves crash against the shore, one right after the other. They never quit. Never gave up. Never stopped, even in the darkness. She admired their tenacity, and the way they didn't worry about what they might hit.

"We buy coffee from the same place," Shannon said. "And I got a flat tire on Monday, and he rescued me."

"Ooh, romantic," Cheryl said with a smile. "Keep going."

And so Shannon did, telling them about Jeremiah

and Hercules and everything they'd done that week. By the time she finished, she realized she had that same warm glow and that she couldn't flatten the smile on her face no matter how hard she tried.

So maybe she liked Jeremiah. Of course she did. And maybe her happiness would win out over her fear.

Chapter Ten

The closer Saturday came, the more nervous Jeremiah became. He slept little and drank more coffee than he ever had in an attempt to stay awake during his sessions.

By Friday, he had Flo call everyone and reschedule, because he couldn't stand to be in the office, and he didn't deserve to get paid if he couldn't do his job.

He walked the boardwalk, a craving to call Mayor Glover and tell him he'd made a grave mistake. There was still time to fix it. The mayor could pick someone else for the Dignitary Award. No one would have to know why.

Jeremiah shook his head and ran his hands through his hair. Hercules ambled along at his side, and Jeremiah finally took the dog off the boardwalk and down the sand a little bit. "Let's sit here for a minute," he said, and he sat down.

Hercules had never complained about sitting, and he flopped down in the sand too. He leaned right into Jeremiah, putting his head right under Jeremiah's chin.

"I know bud." Jeremiah rubbed under Hercules's chin, his anxiety calming inch by inch. He thought of Shannon, and how she'd texted him last night to say she'd finally found the perfect dress. When he'd asked for a picture, she'd refused to send him one, claiming she wanted it to be a surprise on Saturday night.

She had said the dress was blue, and Jeremiah's fantasies started creating all kinds of gowns for the beautiful Shannon Bell to wear. He definitely wanted to see her in that dress, and have her on his arm for the gala. So maybe he'd still go.

He watched the waves for a moment, and then got to his feet. "Come on, bud," he said to Hercules. "Let's go home."

———

SATURDAY MORNING ARRIVED, AND THEN NOON, AND THEN Jeremiah found himself dressing in that ridiculous tuxedo. Everything was crisp and straight and he was twenty minutes early to pick up Shannon. They were still getting to know one another, but she seemed like the type to have each detail exactly where it should be, and she'd likely need all her time to do that.

He pulled out his phone and sent her a text. *I'm ready early. So much nervous energy. Mind if I come over?*

Of course not. Hercules could probably use a break from my nervous energy.

Jeremiah smiled at the message. Three minutes later, he pulled into Shannon's driveway and went up the steps to knock on her door. He'd only been inside the one time. Even when he'd stopped by to drop off Herc last night, he'd just let the dog go in while he stood on the porch.

Shannon had brought out ice cream sandwiches and they'd sat on the steps and talked for a while. Jeremiah realized he was the calmest when he was with her, and he took a deep breath while he waited for her to answer the door.

The door opened, but Shannon wasn't behind it. A woman with the same dark as midnight hair stood there, and she raked her eyes from the top of his head to his shiny shoes and back. "You must be Jeremiah."

"I certainly am," he said. "Let me guess. Shannon's sister...." She had two, both younger than her. He knew both of their names—Cheryl and Cheyenne, and he was going to have to guess which one stood in front of him.

"Cheryl," he said with utmost confidence in his voice.

The woman smiled. "I can see why she likes you so much." She pulled the door further back and said, "Come on in. She wanted to make a dramatic entrance."

"Hmm," Jeremiah said as he entered the house. "Shannon doesn't seem like the dramatic type."

"Fine," Cheryl said. "*I* wanted her to make a dramatic entrance." She laughed, and Jeremiah did too.

"I'll go get her." Cheryl left, and Jeremiah was left to stand in the foyer by himself.

In front of him, in the living room at the back of the house, Hercules laid on the couch but he made no move to get up and greet Jeremiah. So he walked that way and sat down next to his dog. "Did she do a fashion show for you already?" he asked, but Hercules said nothing in return.

Jeremiah's heart pounded in his chest, and finally he heard footsteps coming down the hall. He jumped to his feet and wiped his hands down the front of his legs.

Shannon appeared, the royal blue dress so stunning that Jeremiah stopped breathing for a moment. It hugged her curves and fell in long layers to the floor. She wore a pair of black heels on her feet and clutched a small purse of the same color.

The dress had narrow straps that went over her bare shoulders, and her hair had been pinned up into a dozen rose-shaped twists.

His involuntary functions kicked in and he blinked and breathed and stared. "Wow," he said. "You're absolutely stunning. I don't think we can go to this thing together."

Her face shone with radiance, and she giggled quietly at him. "Why?" she asked, coming closer. "Because you'll upstage me?"

"Are you kidding?"

She brought the scent of flowers and sea foam with her, and Jeremiah swept his arm around her waist, pulling her right against his body. "You're going to steal the show," he murmured, his eyes drifting halfway closed. "They're going to think they gave the award to the wrong person."

Her smile was lit by a thousand light bulbs, and if Jeremiah hadn't already been on the very slippery slope toward falling in love with her, that sexy little grin would've done it.

He leaned down like he might kiss her right then and there—it was all he could think about in the moment—but somewhere behind Shannon, Cheryl cleared her throat.

Jeremiah practically jumped backward, dropping his hand from Shannon's waist and drawing in a lungful of air that was scented like her.

"You clean up really well, Doctor," Shannon said, the flirtatious tone in her voice at a level Jeremiah had never heard before. She fiddled with his perfectly straight bowtie, the nearness of her shooting fireworks through his bloodstream.

"I want a picture," her sister announced.

Shannon scowled and turned toward her. "No, Cheryl. We're not going to the prom." She cut a glance at Jeremiah, a flush staining her cheeks.

"I don't mind," he said. "We're going to get our picture taken together a lot tonight, is my guess."

Pure panic paraded across Shannon's pretty features. "We are?"

Jeremiah looked at Cheryl and then Shannon. "Yes,

sweetheart. It's a gala in my honor. There will be a dozen reporters there."

"You look perfect," Cheryl said, taking a few quick steps forward. "It's fine, Shannon."

Jeremiah reached for her hand, glad she didn't jerk away when he touched her. "You just smile and hold onto me, Shannon. It'll be fine."

Now if only Jeremiah actually believed himself. But he took a step toward the front door, and then another, and the ground didn't crack. Didn't swallow him whole. Didn't sprout vines and drag him down.

He helped Shannon into the car and made sure her dress was all the way in before closing the door. Once he was behind the wheel, he said, "Cheryl is just as wonderful as you've said."

"Funny, that's exactly what she said about you." Shannon laughed, and all the tension between them evaporated.

"It really will be fine," he said.

"I know," Shannon said. "Just sometimes, I feel a little...inadequate. You know? Do you ever feel like that?"

"Every day," he said, flipping on his blinker.

"Really?" The weight of her stare on the side of his face drew his gaze toward her.

"Of course, Shannon. Everyone feels like that."

"You don't think you deserve this award?"

"I *know* I don't deserve this award." Jeremiah wanted to rip his bowtie off and go home. Put on the TV and see if there was anything good to watch.

"Why do you think that?" she asked.

"Because I'm just doing my job. I don't need an award for doing my job."

"It's nice to be recognized, though," she said.

Jeremiah nodded and said, "You're right. It is."

"So we'll have fun."

"Yes," he said as he turned onto Main Street and headed for Sweet Breeze, where the gala was being held. "Let's make a pact to have fun tonight."

"Deal," she said, reaching over and taking his hand in hers. Jeremiah smiled, his brain moving at warp speeds now as it tried to reason through the different scenarios for after the gala. Could he kiss Shannon? Was it too soon? Would she kiss him? Should he ask her first?

He pulled into the circle drive, nothing particularly special about his convertible, but a crowd rushed forward —the reporters, clearly.

"Here we go," he said, his smiling muscles already tired and the event hadn't even started yet.

A valet opened his door and said, "Good evening, sir. The mayor is expecting you."

Of course he was. "I'm to wait here, correct?" Jeremiah asked.

"He's been notified of your arrival. He'll be down momentarily, but yes, we'll have you wait right over here." He gestured to a spot on the other side of the car, where another valet was speaking with Shannon.

Jeremiah got out of the car and made sure his jacket was buttoned before he walked around the front. The clicking of cameras was almost loud enough to drown out the questions being hurled at him.

He slipped his arm around Shannon, and the two of them posed. Only a moment later, Mayor Glover came out of the building. "Jeremiah," he said with a booming voice. "Good to see you."

Jeremiah shook his hand, the press eating up every moment, and stepped back to Shannon's side. "This is Shannon Bell," he said. "Shannon, Mayor Glover."

"Wonderful to meet you," she said, her voice like liquid gold and her smile absolutely stunning. So she knew how to play the game too. Of course she did. She worked with Hope Sorensen daily and probably had dealt with dozens of bridezillas over the years.

"Should we go in?" the mayor asked. "We're just mingling right now."

"Of course," Jeremiah said. "Lead on." He cringed at the words. Lead on? Who said that?

The mayor walked past the press as if they weren't even there, but Jeremiah couldn't help glancing at them. Probably a mistake, because they seemed to get louder when he did.

"They're not coming in?" he asked the mayor once the huge sliding doors had sealed the media outside of the hotel.

"Those are the ones who didn't get an official invitation," Mayor Glover said. "We have six reporters inside.

Six cameramen. They won't bother you, though we have promised them all a brief interview." He went down a private hall, where a man stood to push the elevator button for him, as if the mayor didn't dare stoop to the level of calling his own elevator car.

"Right, I remember," Jeremiah said. He took a deep breath, glad Shannon's hand was already in his. He smiled at her, a brief stolen moment, before the elevator arrived and they stepped on.

As they went up and the mayor babbled on about something, all Jeremiah could think was that the night was about to get interesting—oh, and he really hoped he could end it with a kiss.

Chapter Eleven

S hannon's nerves were through the roof, and in a
building as tall as the Sweet Breeze Resort, that was
saying something.

It wasn't even her gala, and she felt like every eye had
focused on her the moment they stepped off the elevator.
But of course they were. She was the woman on Doctor
Jeremiah Yeates's arm, and he was the man of the hour.
Everyone would be buzzing about their blooming
romance by morning, and Shannon decided she didn't
care.

So she held her head high and kept her smile hitched
in place. She'd worked with plenty of people who weren't
one hundred percent happy, and she knew how to charm
people so they'd leave Your Tidal Forever happy.

She could do the same here.

She shook hands, and sipped sparkling water from a
tall, fluted glass. She waited while Jeremiah did his inter-

views, and she made small talk with the mayor's wife. Finally, dinner was served, and she and Jeremiah sat at the reserved table in the front.

It felt stuffy, like all of the air had been sucked out of the room by the important people in attendance. Exactly the opposite of the kind of events Shannon liked. But the food was delicious, and it at least distracted her from the terrifyingly exciting idea that Jeremiah might kiss her goodnight later.

The mayor got up and spoke about the Dignitary Award, and then he presented it to Jeremiah. Thunderous applause met their ears, and then they both stood back as a short presentation was given on the work Jeremiah did with kids.

Shannon couldn't believe the playful man she saw in the video—he could do magic?—and she felt herself slip down another rung toward really letting him into her life.

"I give you, Doctor Jeremiah Yeates." The mayor returned to the table, leaving Jeremiah at the podium. Shannon could see beneath his polished exterior to the anxious man underneath, and she wondered how many other people could. He hid it extremely well, and spoke with nothing but perfection and poise.

He accepted his award, and a good twenty minutes went by while pictures were taken. The event broke up at that point, but Shannon stayed close to Jeremiah as he spoke to old clients, their families, and anyone else who wanted to wish him well.

Once back in the safety of the convertible, she sighed

as she leaned back in her seat. "Wow," she said, still breathless. "That was *the most* amazing night of my life."

Jeremiah chuckled. "You think so?"

"I mean, some of those people take themselves entirely too seriously, but yeah." She turned and looked at him, the streetlights flashing across his face every time they passed one. "You were great. So deserving." She grinned at him, hoping she didn't look like a fool but knowing she did.

"Thank you," he murmured.

"And I didn't know you could do magic."

He laughed then, and the sound was almost wild as it filled the car. "Yes, well, the kids like it."

"I'd like to see a trick or two."

"Oh, I've got something up my sleeve for you."

Shannon laughed, the same wild and freeing sound she'd just heard fly from Jeremiah's mouth. She liked how easy it was to talk to him. How comfortable she was with him. As she quieted and watched the night roll by outside her window, she decided she definitely wanted to kiss him that night.

"Jeremiah?" she asked once they'd left the busier, brighter Main Street in favor of the highway that led out to their neighborhood.

"Yeah?"

She couldn't just blurt out that she wanted to kiss him. She'd been out of the dating game for a while, sure, but even she knew that. "I sure do like you."

He looked at her, taking his eyes off the road for what

felt like forever. "I like you too, Shannon," he finally said, returning his attention to the road.

The rest of the drive happened in silence, but it wasn't the kind Shannon had experienced with a man before. There was no tension, and no fear that she'd said the wrong thing, worn the wrong thing, done the wrong thing.

Jeremiah pulled up to her house and they got out of the car. He held her hand as they walked up the sidewalk and then the steps. She paused, fiddling with her keys as her sister had locked the door behind her after she'd gone.

"Well, congratulations, Doctor Yeates," Shannon said, echoing what dozens of others had said that night.

He grinned and ducked his head, his mannerisms so adorable, Shannon wanted to giggle like a fifteen-year-old about to get her first kiss. Her mouth turned dry.

He reached up and ran his hand through his sandy hair and said, "Shannon, I'm wondering if it's too early in our relationship to kiss you." His gaze dropped to her mouth, and she watched his too.

A long moment passed, and then she said, "I don't think it's too early."

Jeremiah had promised he could go as slow as she wanted, but he wasted no time sliding his hands up her arms and cradling her face as if she were something precious to behold.

"Great," he whispered just before lowering his head toward hers and lightly touching his lips to hers.

An explosion went off inside Shannon's core, and hot lava oozed out to all her extremities. She held onto his shoulders, aware of every little touch of his fingertips along her jaw, her neck, and into her hair.

She kissed Jeremiah like her life depended on having her mouth on his, and when he finally pulled away, Shannon was left wanting.

"Thank you so much for coming with me," he whispered, resting his forehead against hers. "You made the night bearable."

She tucked herself right into his arms, noticing how easily she fit there, how gently he held her while also keeping a grip on her, something that spoke of his desire to have her close to him.

"Do you want to keep Herc tonight?" he asked, and Shannon shook her head.

"No, you can take him."

"Okay, thanks." But he didn't move, and she didn't open the door.

"Do you want to come to brunch tomorrow?" she asked.

"Where?"

"Here, at my place. I'll cook."

Jeremiah pulled away enough to look down at her. "You don't have to do that."

"I want to. Bring Hercules, and we'll eat, and just... we could go to the beach or whatever." She didn't want to tell him that she wanted to see his dog, eat breakfast with him, and then kiss him until her lips bruised.

He nodded and said, "Ten?"

"Ten's great." She fitted her key in the lock and opened the front door. "Thanks again, Jeremiah. It really was a great night."

He curled his fingers around the back of her neck and drew her close for another kiss. This one left her just as weak though it didn't last nearly as long.

"Good night," he said, backing up a couple of steps before turning and walking back to his car. "Come on, Hercules," he called, and the dog came trotting out onto the porch.

Shannon watched them both get in the car and drive away, and then she went inside and closed the door behind her. She sagged against the wood, pure joy filling her whole soul. "Thank you," she said to no one in particular. But she just needed to express her gratitude for such a great guy, and such a fantastic evening.

And then, she needed to get out of these heels.

———

"I MEAN, IT WAS GREAT, MOM." SHANNON BUSTLED around the kitchen in bare feet, trying to get the dough put together for her butterscotch sticky buns. They'd be perfect for brunch, and she could pack them for a trip to the beach too.

"So you like this man." Her mom sat at the bar, wearing an apron but making no attempt to help Shannon in the kitchen. Which, honestly, was probably better since her mother usually set something on fire when she tried to cook.

Once she had the dough proofing, she'd need to get making that salsa verde for the Mexican baked egg dish she'd been wanting to try.

"I do like this man," Shannon said, kneading with more force now. "He's a great guy, Mom. If you stick around until ten, you'll meet him."

"Oh, Cheryl talked my ear off about him last night." Her mom got up and opened the fridge. "Did you want me to make the butterscotch topping for those?"

"No, Mom," Shannon said, maybe a little too quickly. "I got it." She tapped on her phone to get to the recipe for the baked eggs. "Why don't you get out all of these ingredients? We'll make these next."

She and her mother had always gotten along great, so working alongside her in the kitchen soothed Shannon. Kept her mind from spinning around those kisses last night or fantasizing about what today might bring.

By nine-thirty, the house smelled divine, with spicy salsa bubbling in the oven and the sweet rolls baked and almost finished getting dunked in the salty-sweet butter-scotch sauce Shannon had done while her mom asked her questions about Jeremiah.

Shannon didn't mind the questions. Of course her family would be inquisitive. They'd want to know what was different about him when Shannon hadn't gone out with anyone in almost five years.

So Shannon answered the questions—*Have you kissed*

him? Is he pushy? Does he have a job? What do you like about him? How well do you know him?—and hoped she could put her mom's mind at ease when it came to Jeremiah.

She'd just texted him that he might have to meet her mother that morning when the doorbell sounded. Her gaze flew toward the door. "He's here already." She looked down at her dirty apron and thought of her disheveled hair.

"You're up, Mom," she said, untying the apron in one quick motion. "I'm going to change." Because she was not having a fancy, romantic brunch with her boyfriend wearing yoga pants and a T-shirt with the outline of Utah on it—a souvenir from all those years ago in the snow.

Shannon was halfway down the hall when she stutter-stepped and turned back. "Mom," she practically yelled as her mother reached for the doorknob. "Be nice to him."

Her mom grinned and said, "You take your time, dear," before opening the door.

Chapter Twelve

Jeremiah was instantly grateful he hadn't had a card trick ready for Shannon the moment she opened the door. He'd thought about it. Even had the cards in his hand, but he slipped them into his back pocket when he saw the other woman open the door.

A blip of irritation ran through him. Would he ever get Shannon when he knocked on her door? And were they eating brunch with her mother?

"Hello," Jeremiah said, turning on the charm. "I'm Jeremiah Yeates." He extended his hand, and her mom took it. "You must be Shannon's mother."

"How do you know that?" she asked, and even her voice sounded the same.

"Well, she obviously gets her beautiful black hair from you," he said with a smile. "And I think it's the eyes." He squinted as if he couldn't see her eyes. "Yeah, I definitely think so. Cheryl has them too."

"Them?"

"Dark brown. Same shape. Lovely." He smiled again, nearing a victory when her mom flashed him a tight-lipped smile in return.

"Tell me your name again," he said, unsure if Shannon had told him her parents' names.

"Stephanie," she said, and Jeremiah finally pulled his hand out of hers.

"That's right. Stephanie," he said. "Well, can we come in?" Hercules didn't mind small talk, but Jeremiah didn't want to do it on the front porch, without air conditioning and with any witnesses who happened to walk by.

"Sure," Stephanie said. "I was just leaving. Just here to help Shannon with brunch."

"Oh, I'm sure that wasn't necessary." Jeremiah hadn't told Shannon that he usually only drank coffee for breakfast.

Stephanie cocked one hip and looked at him. "I'm so glad she's going out with you. For a while there, I didn't think she'd ever get over Richard and what happened with him."

Jeremiah had no idea how to respond, so he just stood there and blinked, his smile stuck in place. "We had a fun time last night," he managed to push through his dry throat.

"She loved him so much." Stephanie shook her head. "Anyway, I'm sure the eggs are getting cold. Come in, come in."

Before Jeremiah could get his mind to work enough

to tell his legs to take a step, Shannon appeared. "Mom, why are you making him wait on the porch?" She glanced from her mother to Jeremiah. "It's boiling hot out here. Come in, Jeremiah."

She stepped back, and Jeremiah tugged on Hercules's leash to get the dog to move. They both entered, and Shannon murmured something to her mother, who then left.

"Sorry about that," Shannon said with a big sigh. "My mom is funny sometimes."

"Funny," Jeremiah repeated, thinking of the magic cards he had in his back pocket. He turned from surveying Shannon's house to find her right behind him. "Oh."

She eased into his arms and tipped up on her toes to kiss him, the scent of her perfume mingling with something much sweeter. The doubts that had been swirling through Jeremiah's head about whether she was ready to have another boyfriend dried right up. She certainly kissed him like she was ready to move on, ready to love someone else. And for now, that would be enough for him.

She pulled away and said, "So I made butterscotch sticky buns. And Mexican baked eggs, but it's the first time I've used the recipe so I have no idea if they'll be good."

"I'm sure it'll be delicious," Jeremiah said. He was taking his secret about eating breakfast to the grave with him. Besides, this was brunch, and he listened to

Shannon chatter about her family and work while she dished up the food.

He followed her out to the deck at the back of her house, and it was shady and beautiful. "This is so great," he said, sitting at the smallest patio table on the planet. His knees didn't really fit underneath so he sat a bit sideways. He took a bite of the butterscotch sticky bun, the salty and sweet combination partying in his mouth. "Wow, this is amazing," he said around a mouthful of bread.

"Yeah?" Shannon's whole face lit up, and Jeremiah nodded.

He didn't really like the eggs, and Shannon didn't either, so he didn't have to pretend. She took the plates back inside, and he enjoyed the tranquility of her backyard. When she returned, he pulled the cards from his pocket.

"So I may have brought a couple of tricks to show you."

Shannon paused and then clapped her hands. "Magic. Yes." She sat at the table, her attention on him rapt.

He chuckled. "Oh, boy. I have a feeling you're going to be extremely disappointed." A flicker of nerves ran through him. Maybe this would make him seem like an idiot. Immature. Unworthy of his award —and her.

Swallowing, he said, "So I don't use face cards in the office. So these have cartoon characters on them and numbers. There are four colors. It's a Go Fish deck of cards."

"How very child psychologist of you," she teased.

Jeremiah wanted to close the distance between them and kiss her. Kiss her until he couldn't breathe, and then kiss her some more. He wanted to go to the beach with her and lie in the sand, their fingers entwined, while they learned everything about each other.

Instead, he started shuffling his cards. "So it's the basic trick. You pick a card and I tell you which one it is."

He spread the cards out, and her eyes didn't leave his as she selected one. He liked how they sparkled at him with just the right amount of mischief, and how she grinned at her card and slipped it back into the deck.

Jeremiah marked the one on top of it quickly; the oil on his hand would show up in a minute or so. He kept it in the bottom half of the deck, and had Shannon cut it twice, keeping track of approximately where it was.

Starting with the top card, he started turning them over one by one, at a rapid pace. "No, no, no," he said as each one came up. He paused the way he did with his patients and said, "Maybe?"

He looked at her, then started laughing. "Nope, not that one."

The marked card came up, a pale yellow blip in the corner no one had ever seen but him. "Hmm, almost." It was a blue six with a brown bear riding a bicycle.

He flipped the next card, revealing a red ten with a rabbit reading a book. "Yep. That's it."

Shannon shrieked and started laughing. "How did you do that?" She grabbed the card before he could sweep it into the pile with the others. She examined it carefully from all sides and angles before handing it back to him. "You really are magic."

"Well, let's not go crazy," he said.

Her phone rang from inside the house, and she turned that way, the joy and flirty smile sliding right off her face. "Oh, no. That's Hope's ringtone."

"You better get it," Jeremiah said, seeing his afternoon on the beach with her slipping right through his fingers.

"She'll call back if it's a real emergency." Shannon watched the house until the phone stopped ringing, and she'd barely swung her head back to him when the device started singing again.

"I'm so sorry," she said, and she looked like she was too.

"It's fine," he said. "We've already eaten and done magic. Go get the phone."

So she got up and practically sprinted inside—and in jeans that tight, Shannon had just accomplished something amazing. He heard her talking in a low voice in the kitchen, and he got up and stood at the railing.

"Don't worry, Herc," he told his yellow lab. "We'll still go to the beach, okay?"

Hercules gave a soft snort and laid his head back down. A moment later, Shannon returned to the deck and stood next to Jeremiah. "I have to go into work for a little bit."

"Okay."

"I'm sorry."

"Shannon, I said it was okay." He looked at her, the apprehension plain to see on her face. "What's the big deal? Tons of people get called into work."

"Yeah," she said, breaking her gaze from his and looking up the hill. "Hope said it should be a couple of hours. We have a wedding next weekend and something fell through."

"Then go fix it," he said. "Herc and I will go to the beach at the yacht club. You can come down when you're done."

"You have a membership to the yacht club?"

"Yes," he said simply. The longer she stared at him, the squirmier he felt. "Lots of people have memberships to the yacht club," he added.

"It's just...only rich people have those."

"Do they?" he asked. "I had no idea."

"Most of us just go to the public beaches."

"Yeah, well, they get a little crowded for me in the summer." It wasn't like the yacht club membership was expensive. A few hundred dollars a year, and he could get their surfing, sailing, and swimming lessons at half price too.

Shannon cocked one eyebrow at him, and he stared steadily back at her. "You're a beach diva."

"Maybe I am." He nudged her with his elbow. "But

you're going to be late for work, so get going. I'll text you when Herc and I get to the fancy, divas-only yacht club."

Shannon laughed, and Jeremiah held onto the sound during the quick drive home. Without her at his side, his doubts returned, and he wondered if he should be pursuing a relationship with her quite so aggressively. He could've let her come to him when she was ready to kiss him. Instead, he'd asked.

He sighed as he changed into his swimming trunks and made sure he had sunscreen in his backpack. Shannon hadn't seemed to mind any of his advances— except that very first time he'd tried to hold her hand. So maybe her mother just didn't know Shannon as well as she thought she did.

But if there was one thing Jeremiah had learned over the past fifteen years as he'd worked with a variety of children, it was that their mothers knew what was best for them. They wanted what was best for their kids, and they had gut instincts that never let them down.

So if Stephanie thought that Shannon would never move on from her past, Jeremiah had to listen to that. Didn't he?

He wasn't sure. Shannon wasn't a minor child. She lived alone, and did a lot her mother didn't know about.

In the end, he packed the collapsible dog water bowl and a gallon-sized bag of dog food into his backpack and headed for the yacht club. The ocean would tell him what to do, and he was glad for the sparser population inside the club's private beach area.

More room to spread out. More room to think. More room to hear what the waves were trying to tell him about Shannon and her past.

――――――

A week went by, and Jeremiah saw Shannon in the mornings and usually for lunch. There were a few days leading up to the wedding where she was so swamped with work that she couldn't even take fifteen minutes to meet him.

He had a full client load that week too, and life settled into a normal rhythm for him. Working out, sleeping, eating, talking to clients, kissing Shannon. The receptionist at Your Tidal Forever didn't sit and twitter over him anymore when he came in, and he was grateful for that.

Sunday evening found him lighting a candle that would make his house smell less like dirty laundry and dogs, because Shannon was coming over for dinner.

No, he hadn't cooked. Jeremiah could make a few things, but why bother when he could call in an order and take twenty minutes picking it up?

His doorbell rang, cutting off after the first ding and then just making a loud, electrical sound. Hercules lifted his head and then hopped off the couch in favor of trotting over to the door to see who it was.

"It's Shannon, bud," he said, nudging the dog back so he could open the door. Sure enough, when he pulled open the door, Shannon stood there, looking radiant in a black shirt that fell off one shoulder and a pair of jeans that seemed like she'd painted them on.

"Hey, stranger," he said, leaning into the doorway. Hercules went all the way out onto the porch to greet her, and she crouched down to pat him and say hello. She'd never been inside his house before, and Jeremiah held his breath for a moment, reminding himself that his place didn't need to be exactly like hers.

She straightened, and he held perfectly still while she stepped into his house, into his personal space. "Hey." She kissed him, a slow union of their mouths that made Jeremiah's heart fire like a cannon and his blood ignite.

She walked past him and went inside, and still he stood there stupidly. Oh, he had it bad for Shannon Bell, and his heart wailed a warning at him not to fall too hard. Hearts shattered when they fell the way his felt like it was going to.

"Nice place," Shannon called, getting his muscles to thaw, and he closed the door and turned to join her in the kitchen.

Chapter Thirteen

S hannon glanced around at the stark white walls in Jeremiah's place. They came standard on houses like his. She'd painted hers, but he was obviously okay with the bright walls that felt like they belonged in a hospital, not a home.

The scent of Italian food mingled with the birthday cake candle he'd lit, and the weird combination of smells made her stomach turn. But she put a smile on her face and tucked her hands in her pockets. She hadn't seen Jeremiah in a few days because of the wedding, and it felt like their relationship had taken a few steps backward.

"Are you excited about the painting tonight?" he asked, flipping open the lid on one of the pizza boxes.

"Ridiculously so," she said. "I've always wanted to do a group painting night, but my sisters won't go with me."

"Why not?"

"Cheyenne thinks it's too expensive, and Cheryl thinks it's stupid." She shook her head and smiled, her dark hair brushing her forearms.

"And you?"

"I like to create," she said.

"Ah, something new about you I didn't know." He indicated the plates. "This isn't a restaurant. Come get what you want."

Shannon moved forward, the atmosphere between them intimate now. "So tell me something I don't know about you," she said as she opened a container and found a giant Greek salad.

"Oh, you know everything," he said. "That video at the gala summed things up nicely."

"We haven't been hiking or anything," she said. "The video said you liked those things."

"I go hiking in the mornings," he said. "Early."

"How early?" She tonged some salad onto her plate and opened the next container. The heavenly scent of spaghetti hit her, and she smiled.

"Five o'clock," he said. "That's my morning workout. My trainer, Brandon, gives me a schedule and a map and a time to do the hike in."

"You have a personal trainer?" She ran her eyes from his broad shoulders down his trim body to his feet. "No wonder."

"No wonder what?"

Shannon's face heated, and she focused on serving herself some spaghetti without splashing sauce all over the place. "Nothing."

"Oh, I see," he said after a few moments of silence. "You think I'm good-looking." He laughed, and Shannon did her best to join in.

"Duh," she said, hipping him so he'd move away from the bread.

"You could come with," he said. "But I stick to the pirate code. If you fall behind, you get left behind."

"Doesn't sound like something I'm interested in," she said, shooting him a sly look. "Now, if we could go at a leisurely pace, and pack a picnic, then I'd go."

"Let's do that next weekend," he said. "Do you have a wedding?"

"Unfortunately, I do."

"Sunday?"

"I could do Sunday."

"We could ride the ferry out to Three Mile Island. There's a nice hike there that's pretty easy. Waterfall at the top."

"Sold," Shannon said, glad she had another date on the horizon. Because this week...this week was going to be bad, and she told him about it as they ate.

"It's fine," he said. "But you were going to take Herc. Do you still want him?"

"Yes," Shannon said. She hadn't told Jeremiah how much Hercules helped her, because she didn't want him to know how cracked she still was.

"He's all yours." He glanced at the clock and threw

down his napkin. "Come on, sweetheart. We're going to be late for our first painting class."

———

THE NEXT AFTERNOON, SHANNON SAT IN A WAITING room, Hercules at her feet. He'd been sitting up and laying down for the past fifteen minutes as her panic ebbed and flowed. She couldn't believe she was back to seeing a therapist. Couldn't believe she hadn't told anyone. Not Cheryl. Not her mother.

Not Jeremiah.

It was a secret between her and the yellow lab, who once again sat up and pressed his face against Shannon's knees.

She stroked him absently, some of her fears calming with the simple action. Doctor Finlayson was a good doctor. The same woman Shannon had come to years earlier. Everything would be fine.

"Shannon?" a nurse called, and Shannon almost tripped over Hercules as she practically flew to her feet.

The nurse didn't smile or flinch or anything. She mostly looked bored, and she was a new addition to the office since last time Shannon had been here. "Come on, Herc," she said to the dog, who lumbered to his feet and walked at her side.

"Go on back," the nurse said, waving with her arm toward the door at the end of the hall. Shannon held her head high as she walked toward the door, telling herself she was brave and strong and could twist that knob and go inside.

She did all of those things, and Doctor Finlayson stood up from her desk chair. "Shannon Bell. It's so good to see you." She came around the desk, and Shannon felt a kindred spirit in the cute black pencil skirt and bright blue blouse with bright yellow stars all over it.

She gave Shannon a hug and held her at arm's length. "What are you doing here?"

Shannon stared blankly back. "I just wanted to talk about some things." She indicated Hercules. "This is Hercules. He's a therapy dog."

Doctor Finlayson's eyebrows shot toward the sky. "You have a therapy dog?"

"No, my...boyfriend just lets me take him sometimes."

"So you have a boyfriend." Her smile widened. "I think I know who it is." She retraced her steps and sat at her desk. She tapped on her phone a few times and turned it toward Shannon. "Jeremiah Yeates."

The picture had been taken at the gala, and Shannon had stared at several of them for hours over the past week. She looked good, she could admit that. Her hair had behaved, and that dress was stunning on her.

But it was Jeremiah who stole the picture. He oozed charisma and power, while she just looked like she was holding on for dear life.

"Yes," she said anyway. "I'm seeing him." She took a seat on the couch facing the desk.

"And how's it going?"

"Okay," she said, glad when Hercules pressed into her legs. "I'm here because…I mean, I want to be ready for a real relationship." She swallowed, wishing someone had offered her a bottle of water. They used to do that, but no one had said anything. She'd hidden behind a simple plastic bottle so many times, she almost felt naked without one in her hand.

"You don't think you're ready?" Doctor Finlayson sat in her chair and crossed her arms on the desk in front of her. "You haven't been to see me for three years, Shannon."

"I know," Shannon said. "I know." She twirled the end of Hercules's leash between her fingers. "I thought I was ready. Intellectually, I'm ready. Physically, I'm ready." She thought about kissing Jeremiah and how it was the sweetest experience every time she did it.

"But emotionally and mentally, I'm not quite sure," she said.

Doctor Finlayson frowned the teensiest bit, and she flipped open a folder. "Have you…been intimate with him?"

"We hold hands and kiss," she said, her insides starting to tremble. "That's all."

"And that's okay?" She glanced up from the folder. "Because I seem to remember you saying you never wanted another man to touch you."

"It's okay with Jeremiah," Shannon said.

"So you think you'll be able to be intimate with him?"

Shannon had no idea. "I mean, I wouldn't do that until we were married anyway…."

"Have you spoken to him about it?"

"No." Shannon pressed her lips together. "But I told him about Richard. About what he tried to do."

Doctor Finlayson nodded, but Shannon had seen that look before. Even though it had been a few years since she'd darkened the doorways of this office, she knew the therapist thought Shannon had not said enough.

"I should probably talk to him about it," Shannon said. "That it might be…hard for me."

"Impossible is the word you used," Doctor Finlayson said as she glanced at the file and back at Shannon. "Do you still feel that way?"

"I don't know," Shannon said. Hercules got up and jumped onto the couch beside her. He leaned right into her body, half of his in her lap. She rubbed him with both hands and searched for a measure of her bravery. "What do I say? That hey, I really like you, and we might fall in love, but I don't ever want to have sex?"

Jeremiah wasn't a pervert, but Shannon didn't think for a moment that he'd be okay with a platonic relationship.

"If that's how you feel, then yes, that's what you say." The doctor looked at her. "I can tell you like this man. And I think he's the reason you're back in my office after all this time."

Shannon couldn't deny it, so she kept her mouth shut.

"And you're thinking of falling in love with him."

Shannon shook her head. "No, Doctor Finlayson. One doesn't *think* about falling in love. It just happens. One day, things are fine and you're okay, and the next you're in love." She thought about Jeremiah, his handsome face, his innate goodness. Why had he crushed on her? What about her had told him she would be interested in him? Or that he should get to know her? Nothing about the two of them made sense.

"Are you in love with him?" Doctor Finlayson asked.

"No," Shannon said with conviction. That much she knew, at least.

"But you could be."

"I think, with time," Shannon said. "I could fall in love with him, yes." She looked down at her hands again, the secret finally out.

"What are you feeling right now?"

"I'm scared," she said. "And nervous. And I feel like he's made a big mistake."

"Because he likes you too?"

"Exactly," Shannon said, nodding. "Exactly."

———

BY THE TIME SHE PULLED INTO HER DRIVEWAY THAT night, she'd eaten far too many tacos. Just because something was labeled as "mini" didn't make it calorie-free—

or even small. And Manni's Monday night mini-tacos were all you could eat. And Shannon had eaten a lot. Sure, she'd fed some to Hercules too, and she hoped he wouldn't have digestive problems that night.

She'd told Jeremiah she'd call him, but the words from her therapy session still echoed in her head.

You are a person of worth, Doctor Finlayson had said. *You deserve good things to happen to you. Is Jeremiah a good thing or a bad thing?*

Shannon believed him to be good. A good doctor. A good man. A good boyfriend. So why didn't she call him?

She had to list five good qualities about herself before their next session, as well as practice the positive self-talk she'd learned years ago. Doctor Finlayson had asked her to do one quality each day, so Shannon sat down at the counter, a blank piece of paper in front of her.

Across the top, she wrote HARD-WORKING in all capital letters. She did work hard. Around the house to make it an enjoyable space to spend time in. At work, with the brides and the planners and her boss.

She scratched out the word and went to get another paper. She grabbed a couple of permanent markers from the drawer too, and this time when she wrote the word, it was bold and colorful and perfect.

She'd been challenged to illustrate the quality, or put a definition on it, but Shannon knew she was hard-working. She hung the poster with the single word on it on the fridge and stood back to look at it.

Peace filled her from top to bottom. She wasn't

completely worthless. There were people at Your Tidal Forever who depended on her. Who needed her. Who would notice if she disappeared from the island.

She breathed, and it was easier than it had been in days. Feeling much better about herself, she picked up her phone and dialed Jeremiah.

Chapter Fourteen

J eremiah sat on his front steps, so he saw Shannon coming down the street with Hercules at her side the moment she turned the corner. She walked with her head down, that dark hair gathered into a ponytail on top of her head.

She really was the sexiest woman in the world to Jeremiah, and his heart kicked out an extra beat. She hadn't sounded especially upbeat on the phone a few minutes ago, and her whole demeanor looked like she was operating under a dark cloud.

He stayed right where he was on the steps, just watching her and trying to unknot his own feelings about her. Sure, he'd had a crush on her for a solid year, but their relationship was still very, very new.

Especially for her, he told himself. *So go slow. Be understanding.*

She spied him sitting on the steps and she called, "Aren't you sweating to death?"

"It's not bad in the shade," he answered.

Hercules certainly looked like he was a breath or two away from fainting, so Jeremiah got up and filled the big dog bowl on the porch with fresh, cold water from the hose. The yellow lab started lapping it up immediately, and Jeremiah smiled at him before returning to the steps, where Shannon had also sat.

She glistened with sweat, and Jeremiah really liked it. "How was your day?"

"Oh, it was a day," she said, wiping the back of her hand along her forehead. A weak smile came next, and everything inside him softened.

"Mine too," he said. "I have this kid I just can't get through to." He sighed, his thoughts about Camila turning down a dark road. "I think I'm going to have Kelsie and Sunny take her for a while. See if they can't find something that will break through the blocks she has."

"What do they do that you can't?"

"One, they're women," he said. "Some kids respond better to a same-sex person. Two, they do much more with arts and crafts, music, and other play forms of therapy."

Shannon nodded, and Jeremiah felt like a jerk for unloading his problems on her. "Anyway." He blew out his breath. "Too many bridezillas in the building today?"

"Probably," she said slowly. "I was only there until lunch."

Jeremiah's surprise rose through the roof. He'd invited Shannon to lunch, and she'd said she couldn't come. His chest tightened. "Where'd you go after lunch?"

She reached over and took his hand in hers. "I need to talk to you about something."

The hand-holding was comforting. She wouldn't do that if she was planning on breaking up with him. Would she?

"I went to a therapist today too. My old therapist. The one I saw after everything happened with Richard."

"Okay," Jeremiah said, unsure where this conversation was going.

"It's been years since Richard."

"Five, I think you said."

"He was abusive in other ways."

"You've told me." Jeremiah wasn't sure why he was talking quieter. He was usually the one to press hard topics—on someone else. But he wanted Shannon's life to be easy, carefree, as wonderful as she was.

Richard had berated her if she wore the wrong shoes to a party. Or if they were late because of traffic. All kinds of little things that brought Shannon a lot of anxiety, even after they'd broken up.

Shannon cleared her throat, and Jeremiah noticed the way Hercules came over from his water bowl to lean against her side. He really was the best dog to be found anywhere.

"I'm nervous about our relationship," she said. "Because of where it could go."

Jeremiah's hand tightened on hers. "You mean, like...." He was used to leaving sentences open for someone to finish.

"Well, relationships only end in one of two ways," she said. "A break up or a wedding."

"Do you want to break up?"

"No."

Jeremiah heard what she was really saying, and it wasn't good. In fact, the realization stabbed through him. "But you don't want to get married either," he said, and he wasn't asking.

Shannon glanced at him, and he gave her an equally quick look, focusing back on the grass almost as fast. Grass was safe. Grass didn't kiss him the way she had last night before their painting date and then tell him she didn't want to get married the next time they saw one another.

She said nothing, which was almost worse than a confirmation of what he'd said.

"It's okay," he said, because what other choice did he have?

"You're a bad liar."

"What do you want me to say?"

"I don't know."

Jeremiah gently removed his hand from hers, needing some space to think. He tried not to sigh, but he failed, and the hissing sound came out of his mouth. "At least we're not too far in," he said. He hadn't fallen for her completely. Sure, he'd slid down the hill a little, but he could claw his way back up.

This wasn't a repeat of Elaine. Shannon didn't have a ring. They hadn't booked a reception hall. No engagement pictures had been taken.

"Are you breaking up with me?" she asked, her voice pitching near hysteria.

"I don't want to," Jeremiah said slowly. "But Shannon, you just told me you don't want to get married. Where does that leave us? What's the point—in your head—what's the point of continuing a relationship that will never make it to the next level?"

"You're my friend," she said, her voice small and much too high.

"Come on, sweetheart. You know I want to be more than friends." Jeremiah stood up, his feelings all over the map. He knew he sounded like a jerk, and probably just like her last boyfriend. He looked out across the yard. "And Shannon, I'm not stupid. I've kissed other women. You kiss me like you want to be more than friends too."

He took a step toward his front door. "So maybe you figure out what you want and let me know."

"Don't go," she said, but Jeremiah had never felt so foolish. Not even when Elaine had left him only three weeks before their wedding.

Maybe it was time to tell Shannon all of that. So he sat down, a healthy distance from her though he could reach over and hold her hand if he wanted to. "Elaine—remember I told you a little about her?"

"Yes."

"I said we were engaged, and that I fell apart when she left. She had a dress. We'd sent announcements. People had already bought gifts. Bridal showers had happened. Everything was set for the wedding—the cake, the venue, the flowers." Jeremiah took a big breath and continued. "She left three weeks before we were supposed to be married. She said that not only did she not want to marry me, but she didn't want to get married at all." He looked at Shannon. "Ever."

Shannon's eyes were wide, and Jeremiah didn't think they were all that beautiful in that moment.

"She left the island and lives with a man in New Mexico now. They're not married, and I don't think they'll ever get married." He wondered if these confessions made him weak in her eyes. He decided he didn't care. His experiences made him *him*, and how many times had he told his teenage patients that it was okay to simply be them?

"I knew then that I *did* want to get married. Have a family. Have that sense of belonging and commitment. It's important to me."

"It's important to me too."

"But you just said—"

"I'm afraid of being intimate," she blurted out, and Jeremiah's eyes locked onto hers.

"Ah." He nodded, understanding flooding him. He

stuck his hands between his knees, knowing he absolutely couldn't touch her now. It seemed like an hour passed before he finally asked, "Who are you seeing?"

"Naylanie Finlayson."

"Oh, sure. She's great." Jeremiah honestly had no idea what to do, or what else to say. Shannon obviously didn't either, because she sat on the steps in silence as the day got dimmer and dimmer.

Finally, he said, "Come on, I'll drive you home."

There was no kissing good-bye. She looked at him, and said, "I'm working through some things."

"I know," he said. "I can be patient."

She smiled, a beautiful sad smile that made his heart ache. Then she took his dog and went up her front steps and on into her house.

Jeremiah didn't go home. He couldn't stand to be alone at the moment, so he drove downtown to the bar and restaurant located inside the Sweet Breeze Resort. The first-floor establishment served great sliders and played sports on the TVs.

Jeremiah needed the noise to keep his mind occupied and the food to quell his hunger.

I can be patient.

And he could. Jeremiah was the epitome of patience. He'd worked with kids for months before they'd even said a word to him. He could wait for Shannon to work through some things. She'd held his hand. Tucked her arm in his. Kissed him.

And wow, when she kissed him....

Jeremiah drank half of his soda to cool himself down. Shannon was already being intimate with him, and she just didn't know it. Naylanie was a good therapist, and she'd help Shannon figure out what she wanted.

All Jeremiah could do now was hope and pray that what Shannon wanted was…him.

———

"You're killing it today," Brandon said, watching Jeremiah lift weights. "You've already had the gala. What's chasing you?"

Jeremiah grunted, not wanting to get into a personal conversation during his workout. In fact, the harder he pushed himself, the less he had to think about Shannon and how they hadn't spoken—not even through text—for three days.

She was definitely going to break up with him, and there was nothing Jeremiah could do about it.

He knew a victim's psyche better than most, and it wasn't always rational, but it should always be listened to. And if she had doubts, or feelings, or fears, they were real and valid. And he simply needed to give her time.

"So just one more set," Brandon said. "And then you can get on the treadmill for a while."

"I'm going hiking," Jeremiah said, putting the dumbbells down without doing the extra set. He didn't have to explain anything to Brandon. He'd still get paid, whether

Jeremiah walked or ran on the treadmill or if he hiked up to Waipi'o Valley.

He wiped his face with a towel and tossed it in the bin as he went into the locker room. He didn't really have time to drive all the way out the eastern side of the island that morning, but he wanted to.

His phone chimed, and his stupid heart leapt in anticipation that it might be Shannon. But it was Brandon, who'd said *Let's beach run tomorrow. Six o'clock?*

Sure, Jeremiah sent back, though he hated running in loose sand. It felt like he was getting nowhere, and he usually broke a sweat before he'd finished stretching. But whatever. He'd have to concentrate, so he wouldn't be able to think about Shannon. He went home to shower and get ready for another day of work. He didn't see Shannon at Roasted, and he wondered if she'd altered her perfect schedule so she wouldn't have to see him.

At the office, he handed out coffee to his work wives, as they affectionately called themselves, and ignored the bells on the door as they rang, signaling that someone had come in.

"I need you to sign this," Flo said, and Jeremiah bent down to do it.

"And Sunny wants to see you about Camila," Tiffany said. "She's in her office."

"Great, I'll take this coffee to her." Jeremiah picked up the carrier with the coffee for the back-of-the-house employees.

He'd taken two steps when Michelle said in a really loud voice, "Oh, hello, Shannon."

Jeremiah dropped the coffee as he whipped back around to see the woman who'd been plaguing him for months. The hot liquid splashed out of the to-go cups though they had lids, and everyone exclaimed.

Jeremiah stood there while Flo, Janie, and Michelle sprang into action, opening drawers to find napkins and picking up the fallen cups. Warmth seeped through his pants where the coffee had hit him, but he couldn't look away from Shannon.

She wore a pair of black slacks and a short-sleeved sweater the color of ripe Granny Smith apple skins.

"Good morning, everyone," she said as if she were a diplomat and she'd been thrown to the enemy's wolves. "Doctor Yeates, can I speak with you for a moment?" She turned and walked away before he could answer.

And he couldn't move. He told himself to get in gear and get over to her side, breathe in that delicious perfume, and try to make everything right with them before she left.

Instead, he just stood there until Flo practically shoved him, the words, "Go on, Doctor. She wants to speak with you," coming through clenched teeth.

Chapter Fifteen

Shannon felt like someone had taken all of her vital organs, rubber banded them together, twisted everything up, and then let go. Everything quaked, and she hated that there were four other women only a dozen feet away, watching.

Jeremiah finally came up beside her, and she blurted, "I'm sorry."

He didn't look mad. Or frustrated. Watching him interact with his staff by passing out coffee and signing forms was one of the sexiest things she'd seen, and she didn't even know why. He wore a suit, as always, and he smelled like pine trees and sea air.

She moved closer to him, because she craved his touch. She couldn't believe it, but she did. She wanted to be near him, and she wanted him to hold her hand so she'd calm down. Hercules had been a good friend this week, but he was a poor substitute for his owner.

"You don't have to be sorry," he said.

"Why haven't you been texting me?" she asked, hating the hint of a whine in her voice.

"Shannon, I thought it was pretty clear that the ball was in your court. I said I could be patient. That was me being patient."

He didn't sound super patient at the moment, but she supposed he had interrupted his busy morning. "Okay," she said, drawing in a big breath. "So this is me bouncing the ball back to you. Can you go to lunch today?"

He finally looked at her, and she let herself dive right into those ocean-blue eyes. "Let me talk to Flo for a second."

"You don't know your schedule?" Oh, how easy it was to slip right back into flirting with him.

"I know my schedule," he said. "And lunch will probably work if we can go early. Like, eleven o'clock early, and I have to be back by noon."

"I can do eleven," Shannon said, hope blooming in her chest. "Can we go to The Lunch Spot? It's Thursday, and they have crab bisque on Thursdays."

Jeremiah smiled, and everything that had been missing in Shannon's life these past few days returned. "Sure," he said. "We can go to The Lunch Spot."

"Great, I'll meet you outside at eleven." She stretched up and pressed her lips to his cheek, the way she'd done a few weeks ago when they'd first started seeing each other. He put his hand on her waist and held her there, and the moment was one of the most tender she'd experienced with him.

Then he fell back a step, cleared his throat, and said, "See you then," before walking back over to the reception area.

Shannon practically danced out of his office and down the boardwalk a few yards to Your Tidal Forever. She'd spent the last few days of lunches with Riley and then Charlotte, who had plenty of stories to tell about her husband, Dawson.

Charlotte had come to Getaway Bay after a nasty divorce, and she knew all about needing time to figure things out before a real relationship could begin. Shannon had taken comfort in knowing that someone else had tread the same path she was on and come out victorious.

"He said yes," she practically yelled when she entered the building. Inside Charlotte's office, a chair scraped, and a few seconds later, the blonde appeared in the doorway.

"He said yes?" She looked from Riley to Shannon, who bounced on the balls of her feet.

"We're going to The Lunch Spot at eleven. He has to be back by noon."

"I told you he wasn't mad at you," Riley said.

"Oh, girl, he *likes* you," Charlotte said.

Shannon grinned and went over to hug her friends. "Thank you for helping me with this," she said. "I just… sometimes I can't trust my own thoughts."

"Does he have any single friends?" Riley asked, and not for the first time. "You keep saying you'll ask him, but you never do."

"Riley, if you need a date, you should've come to me," Charlotte said. "There's this new pilot that works with Dawson, and he is *gorgeous.*"

"Really?" Riley asked, and Charlotte nodded. "Let me go get his number." She clicked herself and her heels back into her office, and Shannon shrugged at Riley.

"I keep forgetting. I have a lot on my mind when I'm with Jeremiah."

"Right," Riley said dryly. "I think you're too busy kissing him." She grinned at Shannon, who hitched her smile in place as she walked toward the hall. No, she had not told her friends everything—that was why she paid a professional therapist. But her friends had been very helpful in pointing her in the right direction, which ironically was the same one Doctor Finlayson wanted her to go in.

Conversation. Have a conversation about it, Shannon.

Talking about serious things was not easy for Shannon, though she wanted to do better. She settled at her desk, realizing that she had a ten-thirty conference call with a paper supply manager on the island of Lanai.

She could complete the call in thirty minutes—if she had a strict agenda. So she set to work to make one of those, because she was *not* missing this lunch date with Jeremiah.

At 11:05, she hurried down the hall toward the front

entrance of the building, her thumbs flying over her phone. She sent the text, surprised to hear Jeremiah's notification echo right back to her.

She found him in the reception area, bent over a table with Riley. "Hmm," he said, pulling his phone from his pocket. "I think this one."

The simplicity of him being there, of helping Riley choose a stationery for the company party invitations, got Shannon's pulse pounding.

"Hey," she said as he started reading her text. "Sorry I'm late. Conference call went over."

"It's fine," he said, and Shannon wondered what it would take to ruffle him. Maybe she didn't want to know. She had seen him upset a few days ago, and she hadn't liked it.

"Be back later," she called to Riley, and she and Jeremiah went outside. "Wow, it's hot," she said.

"You're having an outdoor company party in July," he said. "And you think it's hot now?" He chuckled and shook his head. "I think I'm going to be out of town that week, by the way."

"You are not," she said, bumping into him with her hip and laughing. "And you're coming to that party. I went to that swanky gala with you."

"You loved that 'swanky gala'," he said, reaching for and securing her hand in his. The moment sobered, and he asked, "This is okay?"

"Yes," she said with conviction. "And so is this." She

darted in front of him and practically threw herself into his arms so they could share a kiss.

He moved carefully, slowly, like he didn't want to scare her off or break her. Part of Shannon liked it, and the other part wanted him to be able to act naturally. Maybe this was natural for him.

"Mm," he said, keeping his eyes closed after she pulled away. "I've missed you, Shannon."

"I missed you too, Jeremiah," she whispered.

"Okay," he said, starting forward again. "Something light for conversation today. Our game of Things We Don't Know. You go first."

"I don't like tapioca pudding."

"That's because it's disgusting." Jeremiah laughed, the sound as magical as his touch in healing Shannon's soul.

"Your turn," she said.

"I learned all my magic tricks from an online workshop," he said.

"Wait a minute," she said. "You mean you're not really a wizard?"

He chuckled and shook his head. "Sorry to disappoint you."

"Wow." She swung their hands a little exuberantly. "I had no idea you could be so deceptive."

"Your turn," he said.

"I hate the color red," she said. "I won't even use it when I decorate for Christmas. It's all blue and silver and gold at my house."

"Fascinating," he said. "I think you're beautiful."

Shannon's heartbeat jumped up into her throat. "That doesn't count," she managed to say through a wad of emotion. "I already knew that."

"Did you?" He cut her a look out of the corner of his eye. "What about this one? I like you just how you are."

"Stop it," she said, half playfully and half serious. "You'll make me cry, and we're almost to The Lunch Spot."

"Fine, just one more. I'll wait as long as it takes to be with you, Shannon, because I'm falling in love with you."

She stopped walking, unable to think, and breathe, and process his words at the same time. Her emotions spiraled up like they were on that roller coaster again, and she swiped at her eyes when she felt the moisture there.

"Jeremiah," she said, and he reached over and tucked her hair behind her ear. He'd done it a few times in the past, and each time was so full of adoration and caring that Shannon could feel it way down deep in her soul.

"Too heavy for lunch conversation," he said. "I'm sorry. How about this one? I've only been to the Mainland once, and I'd love to go to New York City for Christmas." He started walking again, a little slower than before, and Shannon simply went with him, the game apparently over.

She couldn't speak to continue the game anyway, because what she wanted to say was trapped behind her fear. *I'm falling in love with you too.*

AN ALARM WENT OFF ON SHANNON'S PHONE, AND SHE looked up from the ledger where she'd been working for twenty minutes. She'd taken to segmenting her tasks so she didn't spend too much time on some and not enough on others.

May was the craziest month of the year—well, besides November—what with the eleven June weddings on the calendar. And the Poulson wedding was going to come in right under budget, thank you very much.

Shannon had negotiated a deal with a new paper supplier that had saved Your Tidal Forever almost ten percent in stationary and announcement costs. She'd never seen Hope so happy, and Shannon's confidence had grown with each success she'd achieved this month.

And now she needed to move on to the Keller file so everyone would be ready for the final consultation that afternoon.

She closed her budgeting ledger on the computer and spun around to dig through the physical files for the Keller's. Her stomach growled, but she still had an hour to go before Jeremiah would saunter into the building and whisk her off for sixty minutes of eating, laughing, and kissing.

They'd worked out a nice schedule over the past month, where they got together for lunch a few times a week as their schedules allowed. And every evening found them walking together, one of them holding a loose leash on Hercules.

Shannon had seen more sunsets in the past few weeks than she ever had, and she didn't mind leaning into Jeremiah's strong chest as the last of the light drained from the day. Then they'd walk Hercules home in the twilight, kiss under her porch lights, and do it all again the next day.

He had been patient and kind about her issues, and she'd been seeing Doctor Finlayson twice a week. Shannon almost felt like herself again, and she was starting to imagine what her own wedding would be like.

Her buzzer sounded, and then Riley said, "Jeremiah's here."

"Already?" Shannon asked, glancing at the clock. She easily had another hour of work to do before she could take a break.

"He's coming back."

Shannon tried to speed-read the rest of the file she'd already spent sixty minutes on.

"Hey," he said easily, taking the chair in front of her desk. Hardly anyone but him sat there, and Shannon snapped the file closed.

She put her arms over the folder and smiled at him. "I'm so sorry, but I'm going to have to cancel lunch."

His face fell for a moment, but he recovered quickly. "All right. Want me to bring you something back?"

"Where are you going?"

He shrugged and said, "Wherever."

"You know what I like."

"Shannon." Hope appeared in the doorway to her office. "Oh, hello, Jeremiah."

"Hey," he said, standing. "I'll see you later, Shannon." He walked away without looking back, and Shannon's attention was divided between watching him leave and wanting to do whatever Hope needed her to do.

"I didn't mean to interrupt," Hope said.

"It's fine," Shannon said, shaking herself. "I've been over the Keller file, and I'm set to pick up the cookies at two."

"Great," Hope said. "I want you to run the meeting too." She gave Shannon a smile, but Shannon's insides shook.

"Me?"

"You're ready." Hope gestured for her to come into the office. "And I have a new client I want you to take the lead on. Start with them. Go through every step with them, from beginning to end."

Shannon knew what all of the pieces were to plan a wedding, but she'd never taken on a single bride and seen to every little detail from start to finish. A new level of excitement bubbled up inside her, and she hurried to follow Hope into her office to learn who her first real client would be.

Chapter Sixteen

Jeremiah pushed the lawn mower around his parents' yard, thinking a few steps ahead to get the job done. He didn't edge every week, but he'd skipped it last week so he could take Shannon to dinner. He'd have to get the weed eater out and make sure everything was neat and trim.

Besides, he wasn't seeing Shannon that night. Or much at all lately. She'd broken their last three lunch dates, and while they used to walk Hercules every evening together, she'd begged out of the last two.

So he hadn't seen her for three days now, and his heart felt like it might be made of lead. The smell of oil and gasoline filled his nostrils, along with the scent of flowers and freshly cut grass, and sweat poured down his face as he worked.

Afterward, he trimmed and weeded and cleaned up all the tools. Back in the house, he bent over the sink, cold water pouring out of the faucet and into his hands. He scrubbed them clean and then doused his face with the icy liquid, simultaneously flinching away from the cold and absolutely relieved as it cooled him down.

He exhaled and toweled his face as his mother came inside. "Lawn looks amazing, Jeremiah."

"It's so hot out there," he said in response.

His mother frowned and reached up to touch his hair. "You need a haircut."

"Oh, it's fine," he said.

"Sit," she commanded, pointing to a barstool. "I'll get the clippers." She bustled off before he could argue again. In the end, she'd win, so he did as she said and sat down. It took her longer than usual to get the drape and the clippers, but she did eventually return to the kitchen.

"How's Shannon?" she asked as she tossed the drape around him.

"She's great," he said, a note of falseness in his voice. Hopefully, his mother wouldn't hear it, but Jeremiah knew his mom.

She didn't say anything, and the clippers started buzzing. She worked on the back and sides of his head before turning off the clippers and reaching for the scissors. "Things not going well with Shannon?"

Jeremiah sighed, but he couldn't exactly say things were going how he'd like. "She's really busy right now," he said, the same thing he'd been telling himself for a week now. "Lots of weddings, and her boss is training her to run the business."

He felt tired in every muscle and joint, but he sat straight and let his mother finish the haircut. He didn't want to talk about Shannon, and thankfully, his mother pulled out a large pan of chicken cordon bleu. "Are you hungry?"

"Am I ever not hungry?" Jeremiah grinned at her and placed a kiss on her cheek. "Thanks for the haircut, Mom."

She smiled and started working to heat up the food. "You can go wake up your father."

"Wake him up?" Jeremiah looked at the microwave, which said it was almost six-thirty. "Isn't it a little late for a nap?" And he couldn't believe the lawn mowing and trimming hadn't woken his father. "Is he not feeling well?"

"Oh, the Palmer's dog barks all night long," his mom said. "He keeps saying he can't sleep, and then he naps for hours in the afternoon."

"I'll go get him up then." Jeremiah walked down the hall and knocked lightly on the door at the back of the house. "Dad?"

"I'm up," a voice croaked from behind the door. Jeremiah entered the bedroom and found his dad sitting on the edge of the bed. "I'm going to call the city about that dog." He yawned, and Jeremiah moved to sit next to him.

"You should get some earplugs, Dad," he said. "And blow a fan. Then you won't be able to hear that dog."

Hercules came into the room, and Jeremiah had forgotten he was even there. He reached over to pat the dog's head, and his dad did too. "You can keep him tonight if you want," Jeremiah said.

"You and Shannon aren't walking him?"

"Not tonight." Jeremiah stood up. "Mom's heating up leftovers, so come eat with us." He left his father to finish waking up, and then he came out to the kitchen with Hercules. They sat down to eat, and thankfully the conversation moved onto something besides Shannon.

Jeremiah wished his thoughts would do the same, but they seemed on a perpetual Shannon merry-go-round.

He had never been so patient before, and he wondered if a person could literally die from how long they had to wait for something.

———

A COUPLE OF WEEKS LATER, JEREMIAH HAD TAKEN TO texting Shannon as their main means of communication. She'd stopped coming on walks with him, and it was a lucky week if they got together for lunch.

He'd even stopped bringing back salads and tacos for her. It was like their relationship had slid backward a couple of miles, and Jeremiah had no idea what to do about it.

But this afternoon, he was definitely going to see her, because it was the first ever Your Tidal Forever company picnic. He'd been invited, and Shannon had sent him no less than six texts that morning.

His own excitement felt like it was electricity buzzing

through his bloodstream, and he double-checked the buttons on his polo to make sure everything looked good and that the collar lay flat.

He left his office and stopped at the reception desk and exhaled. "Ladies, how do I look?"

Flo turned from the files in front of her. "Oh, Doctor Yeates. Very handsome."

"Casual," Janey said. "For the picnic." She exchanged a glance with Flo, and the two older women grinned.

"I haven't seen Shannon in a while," he said. "I'm very nervous."

"Oh, pish posh." Janey stood up and ran her hands over his shoulders. "You're handsome. Rich. A real catch. If she can't see that, well, then you need to find someone with better eyes."

Jeremiah swallowed and said, "Flo, you've got Hercules tonight and for the weekend, right?"

"Yes, sir."

He glanced around at the women he worked with and headed for the front door. "See you guys on Monday."

The heat outside nearly knocked him back into the building, and when he breathed, the air felt sticky inside his lungs. But he was going to this picnic even if there was a tropical storm. He drove himself over to the other bay, and around the curve in the highway that led out to the Cattleman's Last Stop.

He pulled onto the road for Aloha Hideaway, a

quaint little bed and breakfast he'd never personally attended before. But he wasn't a tourist, so he didn't need to stay at a B&B.

Aloha Hideaway had beautiful gardens tucked away between the beach and the road, and he took one of the last parking spaces and pulled out his phone to text Shannon that he'd arrived. She arrived on the path leading between the trees, and Jeremiah couldn't help grinning at the sight of her.

She wore her classic black pencil skirt and a bright yellow blouse with barely-there white polka dots. She ran toward him for a few steps before he swept her into his arms, laughing now.

"It's good to see you," she said.

Jeremiah breathed in the strawberry scent of her hair and held onto her, trying to commit the feel of her beside him to memory. "I've missed you," he said, wishing he didn't come across as quite so desperate to be with her.

"I'm sorry I've been so busy," she said. "But come on, we're about to start, and you don't want to miss the Kalua pork this place serves. It's *delicious*." She linked her fingers through his and they walked toward the path.

The shade took the temperature down a few notches, and there were misters and fans making things downright cool in this paradise. He glanced around from the long rows of flowers growing in the shade, to the tables that had been set up for the party.

Everything was perfect, and proper, and perfectly white among all the greenery. "You are unbelievable," he said to Shannon, knowing that much of what had kept her from him was spread before him.

"Do you like it?" Shannon gazed around at the tables, the lanterns hanging from the trees, and the food sitting on a long table near the only building Jeremiah could see.

"It's wonderful," he said. "Oh, there's Riley."

"Yep, come on." Shannon linked her hand through his arm. "You've met a few of the girls at the company, but there are a lot more who are dying to see that I really have a handsome boyfriend." She giggled, and Jeremiah put a smile on his face, ready to spend time with Shannon any way he could, even if it meant shaking hands and meeting her friends.

After all, she'd done that for him when they'd gone to the gala. He had a feeling she'd be much better at it than him, but if there was Kalua pig and poi in his future, he'd do his best.

Chapter Seventeen

S hannon sure did enjoy showing off her devilishly handsome boyfriend. Even if she hadn't seen Jeremiah as much as she'd wanted to over the past few weeks, but some things couldn't be helped.

He didn't leave his clients to go to lunch with her, and her job was as important as his. Just because she hadn't gone to medical school or earned Dignitary Awards didn't mean what she was doing at Your Tidal Forever wasn't worthwhile.

"So you've met Charlotte," she said. "And Riley. And this is Ash Lawson. She designs and sews a lot of the bride's wedding dresses."

Jeremiah shook her hand and said, "I've seen some of your designs. They're stunning."

"Thank you." Ash grinned at him and then Shannon, and she'd seen that look on her friend's face before.

"Shannon," Hope called, and Shannon turned

toward her boss. She stood next to her husband and the owner of Aloha Hideaway, Stacey DuPont.

Shannon's pulse jumped, and she headed toward them, trying not to twist her ankle on the grass. She should've worn better shoes for the environment, but she'd wanted to be professional.

"Hope, Aiden, Stacey, this is Jeremiah Yeates."

"Oh, the doctor who won the Dignitary Award." Stacey grinned at him, and he said something about her husband and his hotel. Their conversation was easy and light, and allowed Shannon to step over to Hope.

"Are we ready?"

"Stacey wanted to say something about the food after you welcome everyone." Hope glanced at the redhead.

"Sounds good." Shannon couldn't help the nervous tic of smoothing down her skirt. She'd been rehearsing her welcome speech for a week now, but it had suddenly flown from her mind.

"All right," Hope said. "You're up."

Shannon looked at her, panic racing through her. Stacey took a side-step and stood next to her, and Shannon faced the rest of the group. Your Tidal Forever only employed about fifteen people, but they'd all brought plus-ones, and Shannon was not used to talking to more than a few people at a time.

Her stomach felt like someone had squeezed it between two pieces of metal, and she pressed her palms together to try to find a measure of control inside her.

"Welcome, everyone," she said, but it wasn't anywhere near loud enough to get their attention.

Her nerves shot up another floor. "Uh, everyone." Her voice broke, and she felt very near tears.

Someone whistled, and Shannon startled along with everyone else. Jeremiah nudged her forward and said, "Try it now."

For some reason, annoyance sang through her, though everyone was looking at her now. She put a smile on her face and said, "Welcome, everyone, to our first company picnic. Isn't it so great here at Aloha Hideaway?"

A few people clapped, and Shannon did so enthusiastically until foolishness raced through her. She didn't clear her throat, though she wanted to. "We're thrilled to get out of the office for an afternoon and just relax, eat, and spend time together. Stacey, the owner here at Aloha Hideaway, wants to say a few things about the food."

She gestured to Stacey, who stepped forward. She spoke, but Shannon barely heard her through the rushing in her head. Her anxiety coiled through her like a snake about to strike, and she felt lightheaded and nauseous at the same time.

"Are you going to eat?" Jeremiah asked, his hand on the small of her back comforting. He steered her to the end of the line, and he engaged in a conversation with one of the construction managers as easily as if he'd been best friends with the man his whole life.

Shannon picked up a plate and started with the

macaroni salad, hoping that would calm her further. Food usually did, as her hips could testify. "Hey, where's Hercules?" she asked. She'd missed that dog almost as much as his owner.

"He's with Flo this weekend," Jeremiah said. "Are we still on for snorkeling tomorrow?"

Shannon's chest pinched and she felt her face fall. "I have a meeting in the morning. I'm sure it won't go long." But she wasn't sure of that, and Jeremiah surely knew it.

"It's okay," he said. "When you're done, we'll go." He acted like the day had countless hours in it, and Shannon supposed it did. But she kind of wanted to just sit on the beach and relax.

And you can, she told herself. They wouldn't snorkel for hours, and there was plenty of lying around in between going out to see the tropical fish.

"It's at ten," she said. "I could grab lunch afterward and meet you at the beach."

"Oh, I don't know," he said, that sparkling tease in his voice. "I'll be at the yacht club."

"The snorkeling there is idiotic," she said, a slight scoff following. "We should go over to Horseshoe Bay. The water is the calmest, and there's the best coral there."

"There's also a million people there," he said.

"Snorkeling?" Hillary asked. "You should come to the beach along Six Mile Road. My family has a beach house there, with a private beach."

"And the snorkeling's good?" Shannon asked.

"It's on a little inlet," Hillary said. "It's awesome for snorkeling or just paddling around on a boogie board or a small boat."

"I'm sure your family is using it," Jeremiah said. "We'll figure—"

"Actually, my parents are on an Alaskan cruise," Hillary said. "I was going to ask some friends to go this weekend, but I'm feeling pretty exhausted after this week." She flashed a smile that did look tired around the edges. "So the house is empty for at least another week." She ladled another spoonful of sauce over her pork and moved away.

"What do you think?" Jeremiah asked. "You want to go out to Hillary's beach house?"

"Definitely," Shannon said. "I've heard her talk about it with some of the other girls, and it sounds fantastic. Right on the water. Private beachfront— exactly what you like." She said the last few words in a singsong voice.

She liked teasing and talking with Jeremiah, and though she should've mingled more with everyone there, she saw most of these people every day. And she hadn't seen Jeremiah, and she really just wanted to spend time with him.

After the party, after she'd paid Stacey and thanked her profusely, after Hope and Aiden drove away, Shannon held hands with Jeremiah and walked with him on the beach. Yes, it was hot, but there was a nice breeze coming off Getaway Bay, and it brought the scent of the sea and coconut oil with it.

She paused in the shade of a tree along the fence line that marked Aloha Hideaway's property from the beach. "Thanks for coming today, Jeremiah."

"It was great," he said. "You work with a lot of fun people."

"I do." She tipped up on her toes and touched her mouth to his, glad he was still willing to kiss her.

———

A WEEK LATER, SHANNON PUT A SECOND PAIR OF SANDALS in her beach bag and then took them out again. She was staying at Hillary's beach house for the weekend, and Jeremiah was going to join her there tomorrow.

In the end, she put the sandals back in the bag, added another towel, and an extra bottle of sunscreen before zipping the bag closed and shouldered it. She wheeled her small suitcase out to her car and stood at the trunk, trying to figure out if she'd forgotten anything.

"Shannon, the beach house is fifteen minutes from a grocery store—and your house. If you forgot something, you'll just go get it." She closed the trunk and got behind the wheel.

Fifteen minutes later, she pulled off the main highway and drove down the dirt road to the beach house. It was a one-story house the color of a pale blue sky in the winter. The white shutters looked recently painted, and she sighed as she got out and collected her bags.

It had been another busy week at Your Tidal Forever, and Shannon was looking forward to a couple of days on the beach—starting right after her meeting tomorrow.

Inside, she found the master bedroom and put her bags on the bed. The kitchen sat beside that, with double doors that led out onto a deck. Shannon pushed through those, the wind coming off the ocean a bit too strong for Shannon's liking.

She took a deep breath and realized there was a patio below her on the beach. She went down the steps to the ground level and gazed out at the water. If the wind died down, it would be a perfect place to snorkel and soak up some sun.

Turning, she found the house had a lower level built into the sand dune, and she started for the patio doors that led back inside. A set of steps went up to the main floor, but she explored downstairs for a few more minutes, finding a laundry room full of towels and shelves full of snorkeling gear, water shoes, and other beach toys.

Upstairs, she heard someone walking, and she made for the steps. "There you are," she said to Jeremiah when she found him in the kitchen with a couple of pizza boxes.

"Dinner's here," he said, barely glancing at her. Shannon moved over to the fridge and opened it, finding the soda and lemonade Hillary had promised would be there.

She felt like she'd been making great progress in her therapy sessions, and while she hadn't seen as much of Jeremiah as she had in the past—or as she'd like—she felt like they were doing just fine.

So maybe he seemed a little distant. That was to be expected when they didn't get a chance to talk every day. Right?

"Mango lemonade?" she asked. "Or cola?"

"Lemonade," he said.

Shannon got out two bottles of lemonade, trying to figure out how to make things more comfortable between them. "Did you bring your swimming suit?" she asked.

"Well, not tonight," he said, glancing at her. "I thought we were just eating and hanging out on the beach."

"You don't want to go swimming tonight?"

"Not particularly." He opened the cupboards and pulled down a couple of plates. He loaded his with a few slices of pizza and moved out onto the deck. She joined him, and they ate with the sunshine and the breeze.

He wore a pair of khaki shorts and a plain gray T-shirt, and she noticed he hadn't brought Hercules. "Where's Herc?"

"Oh, my sister wanted him, and I figured he'd have more fun with her than with us, lying on the beach." He flashed her a smile but didn't really look fully at her.

She took another bite of her pizza, but her appetite

was gone. "Should we go out on the beach?" she asked when he finished eating.

"You didn't eat much."

"We had two caterers in today for samples," she said, though she hadn't eaten much then either. "I'll go change, and we can head down. There's tons of towels and water shoes in a room downstairs, if you want anything."

"I'll go take a look."

"All right." She trailed her fingers along his shoulders as she moved back inside, and she thrilled at the warmth seeping through his T-shirt. "I'll meet you down there."

Shannon took several minutes changing into her swimming suit, though she wasn't going to swim either. She pulled a bright pink sundress over that, hoping it was flirty and fun and said *I'm sorry for whatever I did. Please forgive me. Kiss me.*

She brushed her hands down her stomach and turned to look at herself from the back. It would have to do. She put on a pair of sandals and went downstairs to get a couple of towels and a blanket before she went outside.

Jeremiah stood several paces away, his back to her, and she approached him cautiously. "Hey," she said, shifting everything she held so she could link her arm through his. "You ready?"

The sun had already started to sink toward the horizon though it wouldn't be dark for hours.

"Yeah," he said. He walked about halfway to the

water and spread out a blanket. She spread hers on top of it, and she rolled up her towels and used them like pillows before she laid down.

"This is nice," he said, exhaling, and Shannon finally felt him relax. "I've really missed you the past several weeks."

"I know," she said. "I'm really sorry. My job is kind of intense sometimes."

"Yeah."

Shannon's fear blipped through her. "Jeremiah, are we okay?"

"I don't know, Shannon. You tell me."

She suddenly felt like she was sitting in the black leather chair opposite of Doctor Finlayson, and she didn't like that. Not one little bit.

"You seem angry with me," she said.

"Why would you think that?"

Typical therapist talk, answering with a question, never really saying anything. Shannon sighed, the perfect weekend before her suddenly marred with Jeremiah's psychiatrist mentality.

"I don't want you to be my therapist," she said.

"I'm not," he said. "You asked me if we were okay, and I said I didn't know and wanted to know what you thought."

"Why wouldn't we be okay?" she asked.

"Because you work eighty hours a week and have no time for us," he said. He sucked in a breath, as if he'd just realized what he'd said.

"You have days where you're busy too," she said. "Everyone does."

She lay in his arms, but she didn't want to be. She sat up and gazed at the water. "So I work too much."

"Can you honestly tell me you're happy with how things are?"

Shannon didn't know how to answer so she stayed silent. And she didn't like being silent when she had so much going on inside her mind.

Chapter Eighteen

Jeremiah hadn't meant to upset Shannon. But he wasn't happy with how things were going between them. Texting a few times a day felt like something he did with a woman he'd just met, not one he'd been dating for a few months, had shared so many intimate stories with. Not someone he'd kissed so passionately and had learned so much about.

He hadn't meant to act like her therapist, and he didn't feel like he had. *Doesn't matter what you think*, he told himself. It mattered how Shannon had interpreted it, but Jeremiah couldn't control that.

They sat on the beach for several more minutes in silence, and then he got up and said, "I think I'll go."

"Already?" Shannon sounded one breath away from crying, and Jeremiah hated that. He didn't want to cause her any more pain, but he didn't think either one of them were up for saying what needed to be said tonight.

"It's been a long week," he said. "And I don't think either of us want to have this conversation tonight. I'll be here when you get done with your meeting tomorrow." He left the blankets, the towels, and Shannon on the beach, every step shredding his heart a little bit more.

The following day, he wasn't sure if he should return to the beach house or not. Shannon had not called or texted him since the previous evening, but he knew her meeting was at ten. He knew she had no idea how long it would go. He knew he'd said he'd be there, so he packed his beach stuff and drove back to the beach house, wishing he had Hercules with him.

But he didn't, so he took his backpack around the side of the house and down the hill to the beach. The sun shone brightly in the sky, and there wasn't a cloud in sight.

Jeremiah drew in a deep breath, his mind blissfully blank. But he wasn't exactly the kind of man to lie in the sun and try to improve his tan. Instead, he waded out into the surf and let the waves toss him to and fro for a while.

He went into the house and found some suitable snorkeling gear, slathered more sunscreen on his shoulders and ears and went back into the ocean. He loved snorkeling, and he saw fish and ferns and all kinds of things.

Shannon's friend had been right—this was a great place to snorkel. He loved how he felt completely removed from the world and yet only an inch or two of water covered him. He stayed out in the water, kicking around, for what felt like a long time.

When he returned to the beach, Shannon still wasn't there. Jeremiah was starting to feel like she wouldn't be coming back to the beach house, but when he went inside and upstairs, he found her bags still in the master bedroom.

He backed into the hall and went into the kitchen, where he opened the fridge to pull out something to drink.

"Maybe you should get a beach house," he said to himself. He could probably afford one—a small one. And then he could surf and swim and snorkel every weekend. Hercules loved the beach, and Shannon—

Jeremiah cut the thought off there, because as much as he wanted her in his life long-term, there was some-thing between them he couldn't articulate. She'd always held a special place in his heart, but he had a feeling he didn't hold the same spot in hers.

And that made him ache. He spied a stack of sand-wiches on the second shelf in the fridge, and a hand-written note that said, "Eat as many as you like. See you soon!" in Shannon's handwriting.

Jeremiah didn't know what to make of the note. It felt fun and flirty, like much of their relationship was. But he knew that wasn't where they really were. Still, he picked up a sandwich and took it out of the bag, his stomach not really caring where he and Shannon were in their rela-tionship.

He stood at the glass doors and ate, washing everything down with a bottle of raspberry lemonade. A glance at the clock said it was almost one, and Jeremiah felt like a fool. Shannon wasn't coming back to the beach house—at least not while he was there.

Part of him argued that she'd left her stuff. Made those sandwiches. Written that note. So he waited another ten minutes, then thirty, then an hour.

When the clock moved to three p.m., Jeremiah collected his backpack from the beach and practically threw it in the backseat of his convertible. He didn't see how anyone could have a five-hour meeting on a Saturday. For a wedding.

What in the world could there be to talk about?

And Shannon hadn't found thirty seconds to text him to let him know when he might expect her?

His anger simmered into fury as he drove home. But he hated his house, only a few blocks from Shannon's, when he was there alone. He showered, and called for pizza, and ate it in front of the TV.

Shannon still didn't call. Didn't text.

So he sent her a message. *You're obviously not coming to the beach house. This feels like the end for us. I'm sorry it didn't work out.*

He kept his phone in his hand, sure she'd call or text any minute now. It was almost dark by the time his phone made any noise, and he looked at the name on the screen, almost ready to just let Shannon's call go to voicemail.

In the end, he couldn't do that to her, so he said, "Hello?"

"My meeting ran long, and then something came up."

"It's fine," he said, because it was. "Things happen." But Jeremiah believed things happened for a reason, and maybe this was a big sign that he'd been spending his time with the wrong woman.

"You think this is the end for us?" she asked.

"Feels like it," he said.

"Where are you?"

"My house."

She sighed, and the following silence stabbed Jeremiah right through the heart.

"This didn't turn out right, did it?"

"Why do you think that?" As soon as Jeremiah asked the question, he wished he could suck it right back into his vocal chords. "I mean—"

"You know what?" she asked, her voice full of bite. "I think you're right. I think this is the end for us."

"Why do you think that?" he asked again, because she'd never asked him. Didn't she want to know why he thought they shouldn't be together? Maybe she'd known for longer than him.

"Because, Jeremiah," she said. "I've told you lots of times that I don't want you to be my therapist."

"I'm not trying to be your therapist," he argued back. "I'm trying to understand. I'm trying to have a conversation." His frustration colored every word, and he didn't want to talk when he was upset.

"Because you're not here and I am."

"I was there for five hours today," he said. "Alone. I felt like an idiot, and I couldn't stay any longer." Jeremiah knew he needed to get off the phone. "Look, I think we might just need to take a break. I need to go."

"A break?" It sounded like her voice had broken, and Jeremiah couldn't stand that.

"I'm sorry," he said. "I have to go." His desperation to get off the phone, get out of the house, get away from this conversation, drove him, and he said, "Good-bye," and hung up. He almost flung the phone against the wall, but stopped himself at the last moment.

He shoved the device in his back pocket and headed for the garage. He couldn't think inside these walls, and he knew of only one place he could go that would allow him the mental room he needed: the gym.

———

HOURS LATER, HE HAD TO BE PRODDED OUT OF THE GYM as the manager locked the doors behind him. "Go home, Jeremiah. You've been here forever." Mindy gave him a sympathetic smile, but Jeremiah didn't want it.

His legs hurt. His head pounded. His heart wailed around inside his chest. He'd never meant to hurt Shannon, but he didn't want to be second fiddle to her job. And he didn't want every question he asked to turn into a national event. He was allowed to ask questions, and she shouldn't feel attacked when he did.

But she does feel that way, he thought. *And she should get to feel how she wants.*

He knew that was true. But was he really never going to ask her how she felt about something? It was a normal thing for couples to discuss how they felt, and why they felt that way, and what they should do. Major decisions would have to be made if they wanted to truly be together, and they couldn't talk about them?

Jeremiah shook his head and stopped by an all-night drive-through, which pretty much ruined the four hours he'd spent on the treadmill. His headlights cut through the dark night as he pulled onto his street and into his driveway. He sat in the car, in the garage, unwilling to go inside.

Tomorrow was Sunday. He'd go to his parents' house and then go pick up his dog—and Suzie would know immediately that something was wrong with Jeremiah. So maybe he'd call his sister and ask her to take Hercules to their parent's place. Then he could just get the dog there when he went for dinner.

He'd never realized how lonely his life was. How huge and empty his house was. And he absolutely could not be there that night. He backed out of the driveway again, closed the garage door, and decided to see if Aloha Hideaway had any rooms available.

The next morning, he woke to the scent of plumeria and bacon, and it wasn't all that unpleasant. He'd gotten a room at Aloha Hideaway and judging by how much light poured through his window, he'd slept in for quite a while.

Which was good, as he hadn't exactly been able to fall right to sleep after checking in last night. Shannon was so close to the surface of his thoughts, and she'd permeated his dreams too. He sat up and stretched, his stomach angry with him for the late-night binging and now the lack of nutrients at all.

He didn't have a bag or anything to get ready with, so he ran hot water over the washcloth and wiped his face. He finger-combed his hair and decided he could smile with his mouth closed so his morning breath wouldn't kill anyone.

In the dining room, two other people sat next to one another, talking quietly. A white-haired woman entered the room and said, "Oh, good morning. Are you hungry? We've got eggs, bacon or sausage, and muffins this morning."

"Yes, please," Jeremiah said.

"Juices right here on the table," she said. "How do you like your eggs?"

"Scrambled," he said, and she grinned and checked on the couple before heading back into the kitchen. Several minutes later, she returned with a plate just for him, and Jeremiah wondered why he didn't take more opportunities for a staycation.

Probably because he'd believed himself to be content

with his life just how it was. A good dog. A nice house. Parents to take care of.

But he knew now that he'd spent a few months with Shannon that his life was devoid of meaning. Purposeless. He was drifting out at sea, and no one even knew it. *He* hadn't even known it.

But he knew now that Shannon had been his life preserver. A ray of light in the darkness. Oxygen when he couldn't breathe.

And he'd lost her, and it was too late to do anything about it.

Chapter Nineteen

Shannon woke in the beach house alone. Of course, she'd eaten two sandwiches in the beach house alone. And cried in the beach house alone. And apparently, fallen asleep at some point in the beach house. Alone.

Her face felt like someone had dipped it in saltwater and stretched it out to dry. She was exhausted even though she'd just woken up.

She had no meetings and nowhere to be that day, so she stayed in bed, her mind reviewing the conversation where she'd become single again.

Why do you think that?

Jeremiah had asked her that twice, and both times had lit a fire under her. It sounded so much like something Doctor Finlayson would ask her—*had* asked her— that Shannon couldn't really see reason in the moment.

She could now, and she admitted that it was possible

that Jeremiah really did just want to have a conversation. And he really did want to know what she thought and felt, so he could make an informed decision.

He'd never said anything about her job coming between them until recently, but Shannon knew she'd chosen Your Tidal Forever over him countless times. She didn't have to skip as many lunches as she did.

And she hadn't had to stay after her meeting yesterday either.

So why did you? she asked herself, already knowing the answer. She'd stayed after the two-hour meeting with her bride because she'd been terrified to go to the beach house and face Jeremiah.

Breaking up over the phone was easier than having to look him in the eyes and see that he wasn't interested in her anymore. And if it wasn't going to be a break-up, it would've been a very hard conversation, and Shannon didn't want to do that either.

She felt wildly out of control, swinging from left to right with very little to hold onto. Pushing herself up, she scooted to the edge of the bed and let her feet dangle inches above the floor.

The sunlight pouring through the window seemed oblivious to her mood, which was the exact opposite of warm and bright. She shuffled into the kitchen and made coffee, wondering if she could just drive over to Jeremiah's and….

"Then what?" she asked herself with a scoff. "You couldn't face him yesterday, and today, you look like someone's pumped your face up with air." Crying always did make her puffy.

She sipped her coffee and wandered out to the beach. It felt like an abandoned strip of sand, and while Jeremiah liked the sparseness of people on the beach, Shannon liked the vibrancy of tourists and families, children and couples, noise and conversations of those around her.

On the way back to the beach house, she called Cheryl. "I need a day at the beach," she said instead of hello. "And doughnuts. And some of those candies from that Korean shop."

"You broke up with Jeremiah?" Cheryl asked without missing a beat. "Why?"

"I don't know." Shannon sighed and gazed up at the house. "Things haven't been going that great for a while now, and...." She exhaled again. "I just don't want to be alone today."

"I can be ready with the kids in an hour."

"Great, I'll see you there." Shannon hung up, grateful for her sister. She didn't want Cheyenne to feel bad, so she texted her to let her know about the beach plans for the day.

Can't come, her text said. *Going out to Lightning Point with a guy named Gideon.*

Ooh, Gideon, Shannon tapped out. *Sounds interesting.*

We'll see, Cheyenne responded. *First date.*

Shannon smiled at the text, then she went back inside the beach house and started getting ready to leave. She had to get the dishes done, and take the trash out, and pack her things. When she was finally ready, she stood on the deck and whispered into the wind, "Definitely not the weekend I was hoping for."

But the sky, the ocean, nor the sand really cared what she was hoping for. They couldn't change what had happened between her and Jeremiah.

Nobody could.

Except Shannon.

———

"WHAT DO YOU MEAN YOU TOLD HIM YOU DIDN'T WANT him to be your therapist?" Cheryl asked. She didn't have to sound so judgmental about it.

"I just don't like feeling like he's trying to get to the root of my problems."

"Is he?"

"I don't know." Shannon kept her eyes on the white-tipped waves as they crashed against the shore. "It felt like it, but he said he was just having a conversation."

"Maybe he was."

"Maybe."

Cheryl never was one to sugar-coat anything, but she'd been very supportive as Shannon had detailed what had happened that weekend. Shannon liked that she wasn't berating Jeremiah, though part of her wanted her to.

"So you'll just call him again and explain everything," Cheryl said.

"Why would I do that?" Shannon said. "He acts like his job is more important than mine."

"Does he?"

"Yes," Shannon said. "He does."

"You said your job wasn't a problem until recently." Cheryl looked at her through those mirrored shades, then switched her attention back to the twins, who were building a sandcastle several paces away.

"Right."

"And you said you didn't have to choose meetings over lunches with him."

"I just meant—"

"So really, the job isn't the problem," Cheryl said, her voice getting louder as she talked over Shannon. She didn't say what the problem was, though. Shannon didn't need her to say it out loud.

It was right there in her mind.

I'm the problem.

And Shannon didn't know how to *not* be the problem.

"I'm seeing someone," she said. "I'm trying to... figure out how to...be better."

Cheryl reached over and took Shannon's hand in hers. "You don't need to be better, Shannon."

"Obviously I do."

"But you don't," she said. "You just need to, I don't know. Be yourself. Stop being afraid. Let go. Let yourself fall in love with him."

Shannon shook her head, but she said nothing. She

didn't know how to let go. She didn't know how to love. She'd been holding on so tight—*so tight*—to that ledge so she wouldn't fall in love with him.

And she was afraid she'd gone and done that anyway.

"I am myself," she whispered, just because she knew that much was true.

Cheryl squeezed her hand. "And he liked you, Shannon. *He* liked *you.*"

The waves kept marching ashore, the way they always did. Shannon watched them, wishing she was as strong, as resilient as they were. After a few hours, Cheryl got up and started getting her kids ready to go home.

Shannon joined her, packing her bag and taking down the umbrella. "What should I do, Cheryl?" she asked as they walked back up the beach toward the parking lot.

"Oh, honey, you don't want me to tell you what to do."

"Yes, I do."

Cheryl went around to the back of her sensible sedan and popped the trunk. "Get in guys," she told her kids as she started loading their gear in the trunk. She finished and looked at Shannon.

"Figure out what you want, and then go after it," she said. "And if that's Jeremiah, *don't* be afraid. Just go get him."

Shannon sighed, wishing she could snap her fingers and do exactly what her sister said. "How do I figure out what I want?"

"I don't know," Cheryl said. "Make a list. Check it twice. Talk to your counselor. Pray. Listen to your heart." She drew Shannon into a hug and said, "You'll know, Shanny. Then you just have to be brave enough to act."

She gave her a quick smile that seemed sad around the edges and got in the car with her kids. Shannon watched her sister drive away, and she stood there with a new determination to figure out what she wanted.

If she could do that, she thought she might be brave enough to go get it.

Shannon skipped her next session with Doctor Finlayson, instead getting behind the wheel of her car and driving for a while. She went past the cattle ranch and out into the wilds of the island.

She pulled off the road when she saw a small parking lot with only one other car in it. She got out and walked over to the rock wall. A sign told her why this place was special, but she didn't read it.

The sky held a hint of darkness as a storm brewed on the horizon. It looked the same way Shannon felt inside. Gray and swirling and like anything could happen in any moment.

"I just want to be happy," she said to the sky.

And what makes you happy?

She wasn't sure if someone had actually asked the question, or if the universe was whispering to her, but she said, "My job makes me happy. Hercules makes me happy. My cats make me happy." She took a big breath. "Jeremiah makes me happy."

This past month had been difficult, and she realized now that it wasn't because she was so busy at work. It was because she was so busy at work and that kept her from spending time with Jeremiah.

He soothed her and helped the anxiety in her life disappear. Without him, all the negativity in her life didn't have anywhere to go.

So now what? the sky asked, and Shannon simply stared at it.

"I don't know." She turned away from the storm then, got back in her car, and went back to work.

The other girls in the office knew something had happened, but no one had said anything yet. Of course, it was a very busy time at Your Tidal Forever, and maybe they didn't notice that she was operating under a black cloud.

They all had lives too, and surely they were dealing with issues and problems of their own. The moment Shannon realized that, she lifted her head and glanced around. She needed to get outside of her head, look beyond herself.

So she got up and walked down the hall to Riley's desk. "Hey," she said. "Are you still looking for people to help with that Strut Your Mutt thing?"

Riley blinked and said, "Yes. Are you interested?"

"Totally," Shannon said with a smile. She hadn't smiled in what felt like so long. "What do you need?"

"We need people to walk dogs," she said. "It's a 5K walk, and you'll be walking two or three dogs who need forever homes."

"I've never really walked a dog," Shannon said, a familiar blip of fear stealing through her. She pushed against it, because it was walking a blasted dog. How hard could it be?

"Oh, it's fine," Riley said. "You walk, and the dogs strut their stuff and hopefully everyone goes home with a new friend."

"I could use a new friend," Shannon said, her voice breaking on the last word.

Riley stood up and drew Shannon into a hug. "What happened with Jeremiah?"

"How do you know something happened?"

"He hasn't come by this week," Riley said. "And you're miserable."

"I am not. I'm going to help with the Strut Your Mutt." Shannon smiled and stepped back. "I just need some time to figure things out."

Riley nodded. "The event is next weekend. It's going to be great."

"Are there any meetings or anything?"

"Sure. In fact, there's one tonight."

"Great," Shannon said. "I'll be there." She went back to her desk, her step lighter than it had been in a while.

She did go to the meeting that night, and she met a

wonderful springer spaniel named Birdy. She didn't pull on the leash at all, but she was afraid of almost everything they passed as they walked.

Shannon enjoyed her time outside, though it was hot, and she listened to the woman talk about the adoption process so the walkers would be able to help anyone who had questions. When she went to bed that night, Shannon felt like she'd actually done something good that day.

The mornings and evenings until the Strut Your Mutt event passed, each one seemingly slower than the last. Shannon wanted to text Jeremiah and tell him about the event. Mention that she was considering adopting her own dog. Wondered if maybe he had any advice.

But she didn't send him any messages. She wanted to be able to be completely honest with him when she talked to him again, and she wasn't sure she was ready to do that yet.

So she showed up bright and early on Saturday morning, dressed in her yoga pants and pink tank top, ready to walk three dogs at the same time. She adjusted her visor and approached the blue volunteer tent.

After giving her name, she got three slips of paper with three names of dogs on them. In the kennel area, she handed her slips to another volunteer, who retrieved her canine buddies for the day.

"Shiloh, Winston, and Bubba," she said, smiling at Shannon like walking a 5K with three dogs was going to be the best thing ever.

Shannon smiled back, because she couldn't imagine anything else she'd rather be doing. Shiloh was a pit bull mix, who was mostly a smoky gray color. He was sweet, if a little hyper, and Shannon decided to put him on her left by himself.

Winston was a huge lab mix of some kind, and he lumbered along beside her, already panting and they hadn't even reached the starting line yet. Bubba was a white dog about half as big as Winston, and Shannon didn't know what kind of dog he was.

She joined the crowd of people at the starting line, feeling a measure of accomplishment she hadn't in a while. Even though she worked all day in a customer service industry and had done good things for people, this felt different.

By the time the race ended, Winston and Bubba had found homes, and Shannon and Shiloh headed back to the volunteer tent alone. "Sorry, bud," she told the dog, who walked next to her obediently now. "You'll find someone, I'm sure."

She froze, realizing she was telling this dog what people had told her before. *You'll find someone, sweetie. Don't give up.*

"In fact," she said. "You're going to come home with me." He wasn't nearly as calm as Hercules, and she wasn't sure how her cats would take to him, but Shannon could try him for a night or two before committing to adoption.

So she filled out the paperwork to do that, and then

she loaded Shiloh into her car. He put his front arms up on the door and leaned out as if he wasn't getting enough air with the top down. His tongue hung out of his mouth, and Shannon couldn't help laughing at him.

She kept him on the leash as she led him up the steps, telling him, "Now, I have two cats. You be nice to them, and they'll be nice to you." At least she hoped they would be.

She opened the door and sure enough, both cats sat a few feet inside the door. "Hey, guys," she said. "This is Shiloh."

The dog strained against the leash, but Shannon held him back. "This is Fuzzy and Jean Luc."

Jean Luc streaked away, leaving Shiloh to meet Fuzzy alone. Fuzzy wasn't too keen about that, and she ended up slinking away in the direction of Shannon's bedroom too.

"So it's just you and me, bud," she said. "Don't worry, they did that to Hercules too, and he's the nicest dog in the world."

That night, as she snuggled into her covers, Shiloh on the bed beside her, Shannon finally felt…happy.

"Almost," she whispered to herself. It felt good to be serving others. Thinking of things outside her own sphere. As she drifted to sleep, she realized she needed to do something for Jeremiah to let him know she loved him.

But what could she do?

Chapter Twenty

J eremiah rose early and worked and worked and worked so he wouldn't have much energy left to stew over Shannon. He kept Hercules to himself, because he couldn't stand to be alone once he made it home.

Flo and Janey kept giving him glances when he came in, but they didn't say anything. He still delivered their coffee, and life went on.

It always did.

He sighed and turned away from the window in his office. His next patient was ten minutes late, and he finally got up and went out to reception to see what was going on.

"Tanner's not coming?" he asked.

"Oh, his mom called a few minutes ago," Flo said. "Sorry. Things got crazy, and I forgot to come tell you."

"Is everything okay?" he asked.

"She said he had a chess thing come up."

Jeremiah nodded, suddenly with almost another hour added to his lunch. "I'm going out for a bit," he said.

No one asked him where he was going. He almost wanted them to, because then maybe he could get out some of his frustrations. He'd been pushing himself physically by working at his parents' house and working out at the gym. It had been a little over two weeks since the beach house incident, and he wondered how much longer he could endure this loneliness.

His steps slowed as he passed the office building where Your Tidal Forever was, thinking maybe if he stopped, Shannon would come out and throw herself into his arms. He'd laugh, and she'd kiss him, and they'd walk down the beachwalk together, ready for lunch.

Of course, none of that happened. No one exited the building, and Jeremiah kept walking, his hands shoved down in his pockets. It was so hot in his suit, so he loosened his tie as he got behind the wheel. With the longer lunch, he decided to drive out to the ranch and get a burger.

The wind in his hair felt great, and he wondered if he could cancel his afternoon appointments too. He dismissed the idea quickly, because it was much easier for him to simply banish the thought than entertain it. Otherwise, he would've cancelled all of his appointments over the past two weeks and hibernated.

No, that wasn't true. He hated his empty house, so maybe he would've gotten on a plane and left the island for a little bit. Tried to figure out where he'd gone wrong with Shannon. Because he hadn't tried to be her therapist, even though that was what she thought.

He needed to apologize for that, because it didn't really matter what he'd intended. It was how she'd taken it that mattered.

He also hadn't thought his job more important than hers. They both had busy lives; he knew that. He understood it.

He managed to make it through lunch without really tasting his food or even remembering when he'd ordered. Thoughts of Shannon consumed him, and as he set his car back toward town, he forced himself to go over what he had to do the rest of the day.

Two therapy sessions. Paperwork. Then over to his parents' to mow their lawn. Then he'd stop by the new ice cream shop for a cone before heading home.

"You can do this," he muttered to himself as he eased onto Main Street and got trapped in all the lunchtime traffic. And he could. He knew he could. He just wished he didn't have to do so much alone.

He was so tired of being alone.

The sessions passed. He got all the paperwork done. He drove to his parents' house and pulled in behind Suzie's car. "She's going to try to take you home tonight," he said to Hercules. "You don't let her, okay?" But it wasn't really up to Herc, and Jeremiah knew that if his sister even looked at him, he'd say she could take his dog home with her.

As he walked up the sidewalk toward the front steps, something seemed odd about the place. He couldn't put his finger on it at first, and then he realized the lawn had already been mowed.

Edged too. The flowerbeds had no weeds in them. In fact, they'd been newly barked, something he was planning to do later in the fall.

He frowned, wondering if one of the neighbor's had come by to help out. He wasn't sure why they would. They all knew he came every week to tend to the yard. And if his parents had done this...frustration pulled through him. They were too old to be out in this heat, doing yard work.

He hurried up the steps now and pushed open the front door. "Mom?" he called. "Dad? Why's the lawn already mowed?" Suzie wouldn't have done it. She rehearsed ten hours a day and had always claimed she owed Jeremiah "big time" for all the work he did around their parents' house.

No one answered him, and that only irritated him further. He glanced down the hall, but decided the better bet was the backyard. Sure enough, his mother sat in the shade, a glass of lemonade on the round table beside her. In fact, there were three more glasses of lemonade.

"Mom?" he said at the same time his ears picked up voices from around the side of the house. "What's going on?"

"That's what Jeremiah does," his dad said, and Jeremiah didn't wait for his mother to answer him. He caught sight of Suzie coming out of the shed at the back of the house, and the fact that she wore gardening gloves almost made him trip over his own feet.

"Suzie?"

"Jeremiah," she said, panic streaming across her face. "You're early."

"Am I?" He looked at her, trying to put pieces together he couldn't quite see.

"Jeremiah's here," she practically yelled, and every alarm inside him went off.

"Did you mow the lawn?" he asked, realizing the backyard had been trimmed too.

"No," she said.

"Then who did?"

Suzie grinned and nodded to something behind him. Jeremiah turned, and the something became a someone.

"Shannon." He didn't mean to say her name with so much reverence. It just came out that way. She wore a pair of cutoff jeans and a tank top the color of the sky on a beautiful summer day. She was gorgeous, standing there with her waves of dark hair in a messy bun.

"What are you doing here?" he asked.

"What do you think I'm doing here?" She lifted the weed eater, and Jeremiah's heart danced and withered at the same time.

"Why are you mowing my parent's lawn?"

"Why do you think I'm mowing their lawn?"

Jeremiah sighed. "Is this some sort of sick game? I'm not interested in playing it."

She looked at his father and then back to him. "I came to do something for you."

"For me?" He was suddenly so thirsty, and nothing was making sense.

"I've been thinking a lot the past couple of weeks, since we, you know, broke up."

"I can't believe you two broke up," Suzie said.

Jeremiah growled at her, sensing that something very big was about to happen.

"Sorry," she said.

Shannon didn't look away from him as she took a step forward. Seeing her in sneakers was a new experience for him, as she usually wore sandals or heels. Oh, how he'd missed her, and his heart kept tapping out an irregular rhythm.

"I'm feeling more like myself lately," Shannon said. "And the thing that's helped the most isn't therapy. It's serving others. Getting out there and making a difference. And I've learned that I'm happier when I'm helping others."

Jeremiah didn't know what to say. He didn't want to say the wrong thing, or a therapist-y thing, so he just nodded.

"And I want to be happy," Shannon said, still advancing toward him. "So I've been searching for more opportunities to get out there and make a difference."

He nodded again, aware that a dog had started barking. And it was very close to them—in fact, as he turned, he found the smoky gray dog in the yard with them.

"That's Shiloh," Shannon said. "He calms down once he gets to know you." She held out her hand, and Shiloh bent his head submissively and came over to her. "This is Jeremiah, the man I've been telling you about." She glanced at Jeremiah. "I adopted him after the Strut Your Mutt event."

Jeremiah's eyebrows went up. "You did?"

"He's been with me for three days now. I think we're getting along." She smiled, and it undid all of Jeremiah's carefully planned defenses.

Their eyes met, and he was sure she could see every feeling he had for her. Her face softened, almost crumpled, and she said, "I'm so sorry, Jeremiah. I'm not exactly sure where the breakdown was in our relationship, but I want to fix it." She swallowed and looked at Suzie, who nodded as if they'd rehearsed this speech together.

Shannon lifted her head and said, "I love you, Jeremiah Yeates, and I want to make things work. I'm trying to be myself, and I want to be happy, and you make me the happiest."

Jeremiah's own happiness burst out of the box where it had been hiding, and he swept forward and took her into his arms. "I'm so sorry," he whispered, his lips brushing hers with the words.

Then he kissed her, right in front of his parents and Suzie, who all cheered and clapped.

"Is this real?" he murmured, the scent of her perfume, her skin, as well as freshly cut grass, in his nose.

She felt real in his arms, and he simply couldn't get enough of her.

"Oh, it's real," Shannon said. "And I need your help with the line in this weed eater. Your dad insists it goes in a certain way, but I'm not so sure." She giggled, and instead of helping her with the lawn tool, Jeremiah took it from her and tossed it onto the grass behind him.

"I love you, too, Shannon." He kissed her again, deciding that if this wasn't real, he was going to say and do whatever he could to enjoy it while it lasted.

Chapter Twenty-One

Shannon sat in Jeremiah's backyard, her hands still scented like machinery. But it was worth it. Seeing his face. Kissing his lips. Hearing him say he loved her. All worth going over to his parents' house and mowing their lawn.

And she'd been right. The line didn't go in the way his father was trying to make it, and Jeremiah had fixed it and finished the trimming. He'd fixed her too, in an indirect way, sure. But it was still because of him that she'd gone back to therapy, that she'd found a way to heal the hurt in her life, that she'd decided to be herself, be brave, and branch out.

"Well, at least Shiloh gets along with Hercules," he said, watching the two dogs as they laid next to each other.

"Everyone gets along with Hercules," Shannon said.

"I can't believe you got a dog," he said.

"I can't believe it took me so long to get a dog."

"What about Fuzzy and Jean Luc? How do they like Shiloh?"

"Oh, they don't. But they tolerate him, and everyone's getting along."

"And you're volunteering with Puppy Love now?"

"Yes." She snuggled into his side. "It's a good organization, and I feel like I'm doing something with my life."

"I thought you liked your job," he said.

"I do," she said. "I love my job. But it's just wedding planning. I'm not making a huge difference in people's lives."

"And that's what you want to do?" He sucked in a breath. "Don't answer that. I'm not trying to get you to bear your soul or anything."

Shannon giggled and hugged him tight. "I know that now," she said. "For a while there, I was so defensive, wasn't I?"

"Mm," Jeremiah said, not really committing but not really denying what she'd said either.

"I'm sorry about that," she said. "I haven't dated in a while, and I guess I sort of forgot people ask questions to get to know each other."

"I want to know everything about you," he whispered.

"I think you already do."

"Not true," he said. "For example, I don't even know what kind of wedding you want. Or if you'd like to come with me to buy the ring or if you want to be surprised. Or—"

"Okay," she said, a laugh following. She sobered and tilted her head back to look up at him. "You really think you want to marry me?"

"I know I want to marry you," he said, flicking a glance at her and then focusing back on something in the yard. "But I can wait. I told you that once, Shannon, and I meant it. I can be patient. We can take the time we need to really get to know each other. You can plan whatever wedding you want. All of that."

Jeremiah really was the best man on the planet, and Shannon thanked the heavens above that he'd been the one to rescue her from that flat tire months ago.

"I think I want a small wedding," she said. "Maybe in your parents' backyard. It's nice back there. And I'd love to look at rings with you and pick one out together. But then I want the engagement to be a surprise."

"Mm," he said again just before shifting her so he could lean down and kiss her. And kiss her. And kiss her.

———

A FEW WEEKS LATER, A MAJOR WEDDING SHE'D BEEN working on for months loomed on the horizon. Shannon had been busy, but she'd managed to get to lunch with Jeremiah almost every day since they'd made up. She'd been learning what it meant to make time for someone else, how it felt to sacrifice for them, and how to serve them.

And Jeremiah wasn't very demanding in very many areas, but he did want to spend time with her. His love language was a walk with a dog, or a meal when he was tired and hungry. Shannon had learned so much about herself and him over the last couple of months, and when she stood and looked into the sky, gratitude and happiness filled her.

No, she wasn't perfect. She still had fears and doubts, but she was able to talk to the person she needed to about them—and that was Jeremiah.

He didn't try to psychoanalyze her. Sometimes he just commiserated. Sometimes he asked more questions. He always leant her love and support, and Shannon had finally let go and allowed herself to fall.

Cheryl had been right. It was wonderful to be in love and not be afraid to admit it.

"Shannon, have the flowers come?"

She glanced up at Hope's question and noticed the woman looked a little red around the eyes. She bolted to her feet. "Yes, they've been here for fifteen minutes. Riley and Lisa have them loaded in the van. We're just waiting on the final construction to be finished, and then we're leaving."

"How long until that?"

"Five minutes," she said. "I just heard from Tom."

"Great. I'll meet you over there." Hope walked down the hall and poked her head into Charlotte's office. A moment later, they both left, and Shannon went to see what else Riley and Lisa needed.

Lisa, a blonde planner who'd been there twice as long as Shannon, wrung her hands as she spoke to Tom.

"What's wrong?" Shannon asked Riley.

"The altar is two feet too long," she said. "Lisa's not sure they can cover it with the linens she ordered, but there's no time to rebuild it either."

"Then let's go," Shannon said. "We can make it work." She'd ordered extra flowers, and it wouldn't be a tragedy to have a few blooms on the altar to cover the short linens. She got behind the wheel of the van, and the other two women climbed in.

They usually had their weddings right on the beach across from their building, but this bride had met her husband-to-be at the Sweet Breeze Resort and Spa, and she'd rented their private beach for her nuptials.

Shannon had never been happier that she'd negotiated that partnership with Fisher DuPont last year, and the arrangement was the fifth wedding he'd booked for Your Tidal Forever.

The beach seemed to be a frenzy of activity when they showed up, but Tom got the altar in place, and Lisa's linens looked fine, even with the extended length. Shannon checked on every detail as she flitted from flowers to arches to bows on the backs of the chairs.

Lisa did the same, and finally, the two women stood side-by-side, ready for the bride to make her appearance. "It's a beautiful wedding," Shannon said, admiring the pale pink and purple color scheme. It matched the sky on this gorgeous summer evening.

"Hey," a man said, and Shannon turned to find Jeremiah there, his top two buttons undone on his white shirt, and his tie missing. He was sexy and professional at the same time, and a rush of affection for him yanked through Shannon.

"Hey, yourself. I was just wondering if you were going to make it."

"Wouldn't miss it." He pressed his lips against her forehead and laced his hands through hers. "This looks great. Nicely done, Lisa."

"Thanks, Jeremiah," she said. "I don't think that music is loud enough. Excuse me." She scampered off, and Shannon was glad it wasn't her.

She stood and watched as the bride arrived, and the wedding march blasted out of the speakers hung in the trellises. The pastor said wonderful things, and Shannon basked in the warm glow of the almost-married couple's love.

She and Jeremiah hadn't talked much more about their wedding. She hadn't chosen a date. They hadn't gone to a jewelry store to pick anything out. No, since she'd arranged to be mowing his parent's lawn when he should've been, they'd been working through some of their issues and learning more about one another.

He really was patient, and she was a quick learner, so things were going well.

The bride and groom kissed, and a general shout of

joy filled the air, Shannon's included. She clapped as the bride and groom walked up the aisle, their faces simply beaming with happiness.

She wanted to feel that way too, and she knew she could—with Jeremiah.

With the ceremony over, it was time to move into the hotel, where Lisa had also decorated the ballroom and arranged all the catering. Shannon's job was to get the beach back to a regular place to hang out and watch the waves, so she and Riley and Jeremiah did that, folding and stacking chairs on the truck the business owned.

Sweat ran down Shannon's face by the time they finished, and her back ached. "So we're going to dinner, right?" she asked, quite out of breath.

"In a minute," Jeremiah said, wiping his own face. He whistled, and she knew Hercules would come trotting out from whatever patch of shade Jeremiah had left him in.

Sure enough, the big yellow lab appeared in the doorway of the Spam Hut, and Shannon shook her head. "You know he's been chowing down in there, right?"

"He better be," Jeremiah said. "I paid the owner to feed him and keep him cool."

Shannon laughed and tucked herself right against Jeremiah's body as the dog came closer. "He's got something in his mouth."

"Does he?" The false casualness riding in Jeremiah's tone set off Shannon's alarms.

"Jeremiah," she said in a warning voice.

He stepped away from her as Hercules neared and said, "What have you got there, boy? Huh? What is it?" He stooped down and took something from the dog's mouth. "Oh."

Shannon took a step forward but froze when Jeremiah turned and dropped to both knees right there in the sand. She sucked in a breath, and it got stuck in her lungs.

"Shannon Bell," he said. "I love you. I want you to be my wife, and I'll do my best to be a good husband." He held up a slobbery black box. "Will you marry me?"

One hand fluttered near her mouth while the other pressed against her firing heartbeat. "You went to the jewelry store without me?"

"I flew to Belgium without you," he said. "Picked out the diamond there and have been waiting for it to be set."

"Belgium?" Her mind raced. "But you said that was a conference."

"It'll be my last lie, I swear." He grinned at her, that ring box still extended toward her. He opened the lid and said, "I think it's a nice ring. Everyone I've shown it to has agreed."

Shannon gaped at the size of the diamond. She'd known Jeremiah didn't hurt for money, but wow. "How many people have you shown it to?" she asked.

"Everyone except you," he said with a chuckle. "Riley's been asking me for a week when I'll propose."

Shannon took another step forward and said, "It's beautiful, Jeremiah." Tears pricked her eyes. "I love you too."

He glanced at Hercules, who sat panting in the sand. "I think that means yes, bud. What do you think?"

The dog just closed his eyes halfway and Shannon laughed, took the ring box, and pulled Jeremiah to his feet. "It does mean yes, Jeremiah." She kissed him, not caring that they were in public and quite a crowd had gathered around them.

He kissed her like he loved her, and Shannon felt the happiness way down deep in every cell in her body. After he pulled away, he gently took the ring back and slipped it on her finger, gazing at it with wonder.

"Looks nice," he said.

"It's more than nice," Shannon said. "It's perfect."

"You're not mad I picked it out without you?"

She shook her head, having realized that life was not a script. Things didn't go the exact way she thought they should, or even planned that they would. Life was messy. Love was chaotic. But she wanted to live, and she wanted to love.

"Like I said," she whispered, her lips almost on his again. "It's perfect." Then she kissed her fiancé, her mind deciding on a date right then and there.

April 14, the next year

J eremiah pulled on his cufflinks, wishing the ceremony was over already. Shannon had chosen the day he'd "rescued" her from a flat tire in the parking lot of Roasted as their wedding day. She'd said, "That was the day my life changed, and I want to celebrate it every year, forever."

Jeremiah would've been married on any day, anywhere, at any time she'd specified. Waiting for the past eight months had been the ultimate trial in patience, but the day was finally here.

His dad had insisted that Jeremiah wear his cufflinks, and they had belonged to his grandfather, and his great-grandfather too. So Jeremiah adjusted them again, because they were heavy.

He'd been dressed and ready for the ceremony for about a half an hour, and his dad had been in and out of the room a couple of times. He'd snuck in Suzie and

Jeremiah's mother, and they'd both exclaimed over his handsomeness and adjusted his bowtie.

He couldn't wear the same tuxedo he'd worn to the gala last year, so he'd opted for an expensive suit, a vest, and a bowtie. Shannon had said she didn't care if he wore a tux, and she'd absolutely refused to tell him anything about her dress. And showing him? She'd laughed at him when he'd asked, claiming between all the giggles that it was bad luck for the groom to see a bride's dress before the wedding.

Jeremiah swallowed, wishing he had some family or friends in the room with him. But he had his vows memorized, and his family wanted to have a front-row seat for the nuptials. He moved over to the window and looked out, the beach spreading out below him in both directions.

The wedding had been set up to his left, where dozens of white chairs waited underneath a couple of tents, though the spring sunshine wasn't the blazing inferno it would be in the summer.

The minutes passed, and it seemed like every chair had been taken. People were still coming, and they seemed to find places to sit. Jeremiah bounced on the balls of his feet, jerking toward the door when it opened.

"Oh, Riley, hi," he said, the adrenaline flowing freely through him. He gave a light laugh, trying to release some of his anxiety. "Is it time?"

She lifted her hand, which held a leash. Hercules looked up at Jeremiah, a smile on his canine face.

"They're ready for you two. Shannon's just finishing up with the flowers." Her face blanked and she almost dropped the leash. "I mean—"

"Don't worry," he said. "I won't tell her you told me about the flowers." He crossed the room and took the leash. "Come on, Herc. We don't want to be late for our own wedding."

"I didn't tell you anything about the flowers." Riley looked at him with worry in her eyes.

Jeremiah laughed, and said, "I'm not going to mention it to her." He paused and studied Riley. "You guys work too hard and stress too much over this stuff."

"A little," Riley said. "And I'm just the receptionist."

"Shannon's worked for eight months on this wedding," Jeremiah said. "How's it going? Is everything right?"

"Everything's gone off without a hitch." Riley smiled and nodded toward the stairs. "You better hurry. Shannon has this timed."

Jeremiah was sure she did, and he nodded before he started for the steps. He gave Hercules the time the old dog needed to get down the stairs and across the squishy sand. Her mother sat in the first row with his parents, and he'd met Shannon's parents dozens of times over the months, even spending Christmas Day with them. Her father was inside, waiting to escort Shannon down the aisle.

Her parents were nice people, and they'd lived in Getaway Bay as long as his family had. Her sisters were nothing short of a riot, and Jeremiah really enjoyed hanging out with them while Shannon baked something delicious or while they all sat on the beach.

The sand beneath his bare feet burned a little now, and he sped his steps so he could get under the tent to the shade. He walked down the aisle, Hercules at his side and everyone's eyes on him.

He didn't mind it so much, but he really wanted Shannon to come out so everyone would focus on her. She was the real star of today, and he had to admit he couldn't wait to see her in her wedding dress, stepping toward him with a gorgeous smile on her face.

Once he was positioned at the altar, he glanced back toward the reception hall where their dressing rooms were located. He saw Riley's redhead swivel as she hurried back inside. Jeremiah shifted his feet, smiling and nodding at the guests.

Finally, the pretty classical music filling the air quieted. All the guests stood up and faced the aisle, and Jeremiah couldn't see past all of them to the doorway where he'd just seen Riley. She was right—Shannon had planned every detail, and as a gasp went up in the crowd, he looked straight down the aisle to find his fiancée standing there in her wedding gown.

It had wide, lacy straps that went over her shoulders, hugged every curve in her torso before it reached her knees and flared a little bit. The dress was made of pearly fabric that shone in the sunlight, and flowers crowned her head as if she was a princess.

Which, of course, she was.

Jeremiah couldn't feel his fingers as she advanced toward him, and he only kept breathing because it was an involuntary reaction.

Her dark eyes sparkled like diamonds, and she tipped up onto her toes to kiss her father's cheek before he passed her to Jeremiah. The warmth of her arm in his sent fireworks through his system, and his perfectly memorized vows flew out of his mind.

He smiled down at Shannon and pressed his lips to her temple. She turned toward the pastor and Jeremiah went with her. The minister welcomed everyone and gave a bit of counsel to Shannon and Jeremiah to never go to bed angry.

Jeremiah wasn't sure he believed that, because sometimes it was better to sleep on something than keep talking when he was tired. Sometimes things were clearer in the morning. Talking when angry or frustrated didn't usually end well, in his experience.

But the pastor moved on, and Jeremiah paid attention so he'd know when to talk when it was his turn. It didn't take long, and then the pastor said, "And the bride and groom have written their own vows."

Shannon turned back to Jeremiah, a clear indication that he was going first. He had her face memorized, and he opened his mouth to speak, glad his vows were on the tip of his tongue.

"Shannon, I used to time when I'd go into the coffee shop so I could see you. I did this for about a year before the perfect opportunity presented itself for me to ask you out. I'm so glad you got that flat tire, and that you said yes when I asked you to go out with me."

He swallowed, not used to wearing his heart out on his sleeve for quite so many people to see and hear.

"I love you, and I can't wait until we can share our lives together."

Shannon's eyes shone like glass, and she began her vows, saying that day she'd gotten a flat tire was the best day of her life too. She said, "I admire your patience and your determination and dedication to your family and practice. I love you and Hercules, and I can't wait to be your wife."

Jeremiah couldn't wait either, and thankfully, the pastor finished the ceremony pretty quickly after that, proclaiming that Jeremiah could kiss his bride.

So he did, and kissing his wife was twice as wonderful as kissing his fiancée. "I love you," he whispered against Shannon's lips, and she giggled before repeating the sentiment and kissing him again.

———

Keep reading for a sneak peek at the next book in the series, **THE ISLAND ESCAPE.**

Sneak Peek! The Island Escape
Chapter One

R iley Randall leaned her head back as the plane touched down on the island of Getaway Bay. She loved visiting her family. She did. Honestly. But it had been a little bit much with all sixteen of them there, celebrating her parents fiftieth wedding anniversary.

With her four older siblings, her parents, and her six nieces and nephews, Riley had enjoyed a great week on Oahu. She really had.

But she was very happy to be home, in Getaway Bay, where she could eat whatever cereal she wanted in her little bungalow, sleep past six a.m., and have a moment— or two—of silence when she needed it.

She'd definitely felt left out this week, but she knew it wasn't her siblings' fault. They all had a spouse, and she didn't. It was natural to pair up that way, but she'd often been left to herself to find someone to paddleboard with, or someone to sit by at dinner, or someone to go with her up to the bathrooms from the beach.

Yes, she was definitely very happy to be home.

The seatbelt sign on the airplane turned off, and a flurry of activity started. She sat near the back of the plane, but she stood up anyway. Because of her petite frame, the top of her head barely touched the underside of the overhead compartment.

It seemed to take forever for the crowd to inch forward, get their bags down, collect their cell phones. Riley normally wasn't impatient, but she needed to go to the bathroom, and she was simply peopled out.

When it was finally her turn, the people on her row moved into the aisle. "Yours is the pink one, right?" the man beside her said, and Riley nodded.

"Yes, thank you."

He got her luggage down for her, and she followed him off the plane. How the flight attendants could still be smiling boggled her mind, and yet she smiled at them as she got off too. So it could be done.

After all, she worked in an industry that required an endless supply of smiles, even when there was nothing to smile about.

Riley sure had enjoyed her time away from Your Tidal Forever. The stress of making sure every appointment got scheduled correctly, with the right person, at the right time. Her boss was somewhat overbearing, but Riley had learned to love Hope. She loved all the people she'd worked with, even if some of them had gone on to get their own happily-ever-after too.

She just wanted one of her own. *And you'll get it*, she told herself as the line in front of her stalled again just after she'd stepped off the plane. She sighed and looked down, her eye catching on something shiny on the jetway.

It was a watch, and she bent to pick it up. "Is this yours?" she asked the man in front of her. He turned and looked at it, shook his head, and moved when the line did.

Concerned, but unsure about what to do with the watch, Riley followed him. No one grabbed onto her arm or demanded she give them the watch. She slipped it into her purse, intending to find out whose it was and return it—right after she took a good, long nap.

———

Later that evening, Riley had slept, unpacked her bag, and put a load of laundry in the washing machine before she remembered the watch. She retrieved it from her purse and attempted to turn it on, but it wouldn't power up.

She examined the charging plug, and she didn't have anything that would fit it. But she knew who did— Shannon Bell, a co-worker at Your Tidal Forever. Riley had seen Shannon wear a watch similar to this one before, albeit in a shade of rosy pink and not this masculine black.

She pulled out her phone and tapped a message to Shannon. *Can you charge this watch?* She snapped a picture of the item and sent it along to Shannon.

Where did you get that?

I found it on the plane, Riley said, though that wasn't technically true. *If I can power it up, I might be able to see who it belongs to.*

I'll bring my charger to work tomorrow.

Work tomorrow.

Riley was tired just thinking about it.

But off to work she went the next day, as it was Monday, and she'd spent the last seven days on vacation. She didn't think it was fair that vacation drained her so much, but she didn't really have anyone to complain to about it.

"And that's not even true," she muttered to herself. After work today, she'd stop by the pet paradise and pick up her two cats, who had been boarded there while she celebrated the beginnings of her family.

So she could definitely complain to Marbles and Sunshine, detail everything for them about the trip, what her sister had said, and the secrets her brother had told her about their other brother.

She smiled just thinking of all of them, and she was glad she still loved them, even after spending so much time with them in such close proximity.

Riley always arrived before almost anyone else at the

wedding planning business. She loved her job, and she was very good at it. Her desk felt like it wasn't quite hers, and she took a half an hour while the rest of the consultants came in to get everything back where it should be.

Shannon finally arrived, her handsome husband continuing down the sidewalk to the building where he worked. Jeremiah was a doctor, and he and Shannon were a perfect fit for one another.

"I brought the charger," Shannon said. "And it's so good to see you." She came around the desk and hugged Riley, and Riley let the feelings of love move through her. See, she didn't need a man. She had girlfriends.

In her heart of hearts, though, Riley knew it wasn't the same. "Thank you. What have I missed?"

"Oh my—holy cow." Shannon covered her mouth. "So much has happened. Charlotte announced that she and Dawson are adopting a baby."

Riley stalled in her movement to plug in the watch. "You're kidding."

"I am really not." Shannon looked like she'd swallowed stars and they now shone in her eyes. "It was very exciting. Hope brought in cake and then she cried through the whole thing."

"Oh, that's too bad." Riley's spirits deflated. Hope and her husband Aiden had been trying to have kids for a while, and it just wasn't working out.

Shannon's phone rang, and she said, "We have to lunch today and get caught up," before walking a few steps and answering the call.

Riley finished plugging in the watch, enjoying the little chimes it made as it powered on. Now, she'd just figure out who this device belonged to, and she'd have done her good deed for the day.

———

FOUR DAYS LATER, RILEY SLIPPED INTO THE BATHROOM TO check her hair. She was meeting one Evan Garfield today to return the watch she'd found on the jetway. He'd confirmed a few things on the watch, so Riley was sure it was him, plus it had been his email address she'd sent the message to about finding the watch.

He'd apparently been on the island for a concert, and he was still in town. "So you don't need to check your hair," she muttered to her reflection. "He's a tourist, Riley. You don't date tourists."

But she was seriously considering it, as it seemed like she'd been through all the eligible bachelors on the island that were permanent residents.

Still, some measure of hope bounced around in her chest as she exited the bathroom, grabbed the watch from her desk drawer, and headed out. She and Evan were meeting at Roasted on the other side of East Bay, and she opted to walk though the September sun would melt her makeup off her face after about five minutes.

She showed up early and scanned the place for someone who looked like an Evan. Almost scoffing at herself—because what did an Evan even look like?—she moved over to the counter and ordered a latte with cream.

Hardly anyone actually came inside Roasted, choosing instead to use their drive-through window, so she hadn't thought to give the guy her physical description. It wasn't like they were going on a blind date. She shook her head at her romantic ideas about passing off a lost item.

The bell on the door rang, and three men entered. They all wore beanies, which Riley found odd, and sunglasses, which fit the Hawaiian atmosphere. She watched them approach the counter, wondering if one of them could be Evan.

They all wore jeans and some version of a Georgia Panic T-shirt, which Riley found odd. Something jiggled in the back of her brain about the band, but she couldn't put her finger on what. Then the barista set her latte down in front of her and turned to the men.

Distracted by the delicious coffee, Riley twisted away from them and sipped her hot caffeine. The stool next to her scraped, and a man said, "Is this seat taken?"

"It is by you," Riley said with a smile in his general direction. The other two men stayed down by the register, and neither looked in her direction.

"You know that has a plastic straw in it, right?" He nodded to her drink.

Riley simply lifted the little red straw to her lips and sucked on her latte. The liquid was much too hot to take much into her mouth, but she did it anyway, never removing her eyes from the man next to her.

He had a sexy scruff going on, and if he'd take off those sunglasses, Riley would bet money she'd find a beautiful pair of dark eyes beneath those bushy brows. His hair was dark poking out of the beanie, with that beard to match.

"I'll tie it in a knot before I throw it away," she said.

"That doesn't always work." He plucked a napkin from the dispenser on the counter. "A lot of sea animals die from the plastic in the oceans."

Riley had read all about it. "I'm surprised someone like you knows that," she said, teasing him and hoping he could hear it. She'd never seen him or the men with him around the island, and she was probably flirting with a tourist.

But these guys didn't seem like tourists. No board shorts. No flip flops. No long, blond hair. T-shirts and jeans really stood out on the island, and she wondered who they were and what they were doing in Getaway Bay.

"Someone like me?" he asked.

"Yeah," she said. "Someone so handsome and tall and obviously into the same coffee as me." She nodded toward the cup as the barista set down another latte—with a little red, plastic straw in it.

The man chuckled, and Riley really wanted to get his name and number. She glanced toward the door, her thoughts about Evan somewhere way below this guy. She almost didn't want him to show up.

"And your friends sat over there," she said, pointing with that straw. "Did you guys have some sort of bro code or something?"

The man laughed again, his version of saying yes.

"Are you new on the island?" she asked.

"What gave it away?" he asked.

"The lack of swimming gear," she said. "The jeans. The beanie in September. I don't know. I just have a way of knowing."

"Do you live here?"

"Yep."

"Raised here?"

"No, I grew up on Oahu, but I've lived in Getaway Bay for oh, let's see. At least a decade now." She reminded herself she was thirty-five years old now. So she'd been on the island for twelve years, not just ten. She didn't correct herself though. Two years didn't make a difference to this guy.

But two years made a lot of difference to Riley.

"So, you locals regularly get coffee in the middle of the day, when it's super hot outside?" he asked.

"Oh, honey," she said, playfully putting one of her immaculately manicured hands on his arm. "It's not super hot right now. Maybe in July." She twittered out a laugh she hoped would earn her his number and looked at him.

"So why are you here?" he asked, scanning her clothes. "Are you drinking coffee for lunch?"

"Today I am," she said, taking another sip.

"Do you work around here?"

"Other side of the bay," she said. "A wedding planning place."

He nodded as if he knew the spot, but Riley knew he didn't. She couldn't help herself, though. Maybe she just wanted to prove she still had some game when it came to flirting with gorgeous men.

"What does a guy have to do to get your number?" he asked.

"Give me your phone." She held out her palm, victory only breaths away. "My name's Riley, by the way."

He handed her his phone, and she started tapping on it to get to his contacts and put herself in them. She paused, realizing he hadn't given her his name.

"Riley Randall?" he asked.

"Yeah." An alarm sounded in her head as she cocked it. "Who are you?"

"I'm Evan Garfield. I think you have my watch."

Get THE ISLAND ESCAPE in paperback, ebook, or audiobook!

Books in the Getaway Bay Romance series

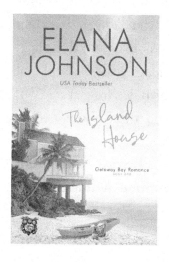

The Island House (Book 1): Charlotte Madsen's whole world came crashing down six months ago with the words, "I met someone else."

Can Charlotte navigate the healing process to find love again?

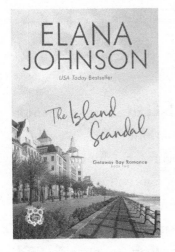

The Island Scandal (Book 2): Ashley Fox has known three things since age twelve: she was an excellent seamstress, what her wedding would look like, and that she'd never leave the island of Getaway Bay. Now, at age 35, she's been right about two of them, at least.

Can Burke and Ash find a way to navigate a romance when they've only ever been friends?

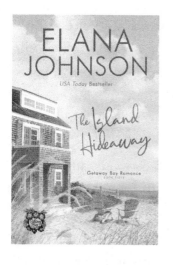

The Island Hideaway (Book 3): She's 37, single (except for the cat), and a synchronized swimmer looking to make some extra cash. Pathetic, right? She thinks so, and she's going to spend this summer housesitting a cliffside hideaway and coming up with a plan to turn her life around.

Can Noah and Zara fight their feelings for each other as easily as they trade jabs? Or will this summer shape up to be the one that provides the romance they've each always wanted?

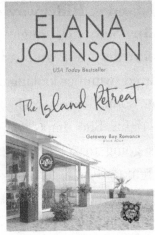

The Island Retreat (Book 4): Shannon's 35, divorced, and the highlight of her day is getting to the coffee shop before the morning rush. She tells herself that's fine, because she's got two cats and a past filled with emotional abuse. But she might be ready to heal so she can retreat into the arms of a man she's known for years...

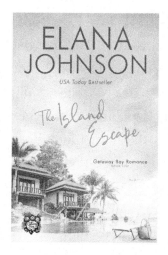

The Island Escape (Book 5): Riley Randall has spent eight years smiling at new brides, being excited for her friends as they find Mr. Right, and dating by a strict set of rules that she never breaks. But she might have to consider bending those rules ever so slightly if she wants an escape from the island...

The Island Storm (Book 6): Lisa is 36, tired of the dating scene in Getaway Bay, and practically the only wedding planner at her company that hasn't found her own happy-ever-after. She's tried dating apps and blind dates...but could the company party put a man she's known for years into the spotlight?

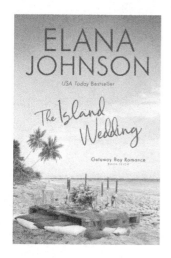

The Island Wedding (Book 7): Deirdre is almost 40, estranged from her teenaged daughter, and determined not to feel sorry for herself. She does the best she can with the cards life has dealt her and she's dreaming of another island wedding...but it certainly can't happen with the widowed Chief of Police.

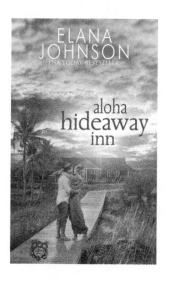

Getaway Bay (Book 2): Can Esther deal with dozens of business tasks, unhappy tourists, *and* the twists and turns in her new relationship?

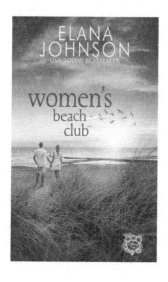

Women's Beach Club (Book 3): With the help of her friends in the Beach Club, can Tawny solve the mystery, stay safe, and keep her man?

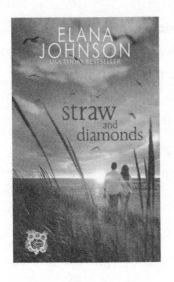

Straw and Diamonds (Book 4): Can Sasha maintain her sanity amidst their busy schedules, her issues with men like Jasper, and her desires to take her business to the next level?

The Billionaire Club (Book 5): Can Lexie keep her business affairs in the shadows while she brings her relationship out of them? Or will she have to confess everything to her new friends...and Jason?

Sweet Breeze Resort (Book 6): Can Gina manage her business across the sea and finish the remodel at Sweet Breeze, all while developing a meaningful relationship with Owen and his sons?

Rainforest Retreat (Book 7): As their paths continue to cross and Lawrence and Maizee spend more and more time together, will he find in her a retreat from all the family pressure? Can Maizee manage her relationship with her boss, or will she once again put her heart—and her job—on the line?

Getaway Bay Singles (Book 8): Can Katie bring him into her life, her daughter's life, and manage her business while he manages the app? Or will everything fall apart for a second time?

Books in the Stranded in Getaway Bay Romance series

The Perfect Storm (Book 1): A freak storm has her sliding down the mountain...right into the arms of her ex. As Eden and Holden spend time out in the wilds of Hawaii trying to survive, their old flame is rekindled. But with secrets and old feelings in the way, will Holden be able to take all the broken pieces of his life and put them back together in a way that makes sense? Or will he lose his heart and the reputation of his company because of a single landslide?

The Overboard Mistake (Book 2): Friends who ditch her. A pod of killer whales. A limping cruise ship. All reasons Iris finds herself stranded on an deserted island with the handsome Navy SEAL...

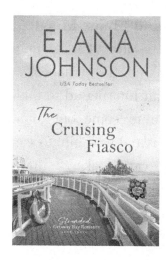

The Cruising Fiasco (Book 3): He can throw a precision pass, but he's dead in the water in matters of the heart...

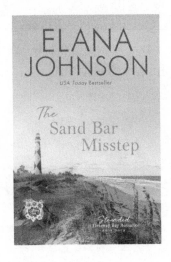

The Sand Bar Misstep (Book 4): Tired of the dating scene, a cowboy billionaire puts up an Internet ad to find a woman to come out to a deserted island with him to see if they can make a love connection...

About Elana

Elana Johnson is the USA Today bestselling and Kindle All-Star author of dozens of clean and wholesome contemporary romance novels. She lives in Utah, where she mothers two fur babies, works with her husband full-time, and eats a lot of veggies while writing. Find her on her website at feelgoodfictionbooks.com

Made in the USA
Monee, IL
21 July 2024

62412954R00152